What if I Loved You

A SMALL TOWN CHRISTIAN ROMANCE

UNFAILING LOVE

BOOK SIX

MANDI BLAKE

What if I Loved You
Unfailing Love Book 6
By Mandi Blake

Published in the United States of America

Cover Designer: Amanda Walker PA & Design Services

Editor: Editing Done Write

Contents

Prologue

LIZ

Liz stared at a loose thread on the arm of Mr. Garrison's couch as the tears dried on her face. She'd been inconsolable when she'd first arrived with Sheriff Tubbs. Now, the tears had stopped, either because they were all used up or because she'd slipped into a numbing shock. She'd heard the mind could do that—block out terrible things to allow coping.

She pried her gaze from the frayed seam. Would she ever see this place again?

Sheriff Tubbs and Mr. Garrison were still talking in the kitchen. They stood, both with arms crossed over their chests and brows furrowed in concentration, discussing the logistics of her future.

Liz hadn't thought much about what lay ahead for her. College hadn't ever been an option, and her job at the library seemed stable. She'd just assumed she'd go on working after graduation, living at home, cleaning up after and cooking for a dad who may or may not come home on any given night.

Liz swallowed past the dryness in her throat. Dad wouldn't be coming home for a while, if ever.

Sheriff Tubbs' worried gaze turned toward her. She stood leaning against the brown paneled wall of Mr. Garrison's living room. She'd never met the sheriff before, but he'd been kind to her tonight. If Mr. Garrison trusted him, her instinct was to do the same.

The sheriff was everything she imagined a dad should look like with his slight belly, worn hands, kind blue eyes, and salt-and-pepper mustache. Even his voice held a timbre she imagined would be ideal for telling stories of dragons and kingdoms and castles.

He was everything her dad wasn't.

Sheriff Tubbs turned back to Mr. Garrison. "Let me see what I can do."

Liz followed the sheriff with her gaze as he walked past her and out the front door.

"Liz." Mr. Garrison motioned for her to join him.

Her familiar tears returned. Not only was she unsure if she would ever step foot inside Mr. Garrison's house, but she wasn't sure if she would ever see him again either. The realization ripped the remaining shreds of her heart.

Mr. Garrison patted the back of a chair at the table, indicating she should sit, while he took the one beside it. She'd sat at this table hundreds of times, but this might be her last.

"I think we're about finished here, Liz. You don't need to take clothes or anything. We'll get you some new things." Mr. Garrison paused to let the flood of information wash over her. "Is there anything I need to send Sheriff Tubbs to fetch from your place?"

Liz bit her lip and shook her head slowly. She couldn't think of anything she'd want to take with her. A strand of her hair had escaped from her ponytail, and she brushed it behind her ear.

"Where am I going?" Not that she cared, but she needed something to focus on besides the nightmares she'd witnessed tonight.

"Probably Dallas. I want you close to my resources."

"What resources?" Liz questioned. "How do you even know people who can help me?" She'd never heard her neighbor talk about knowing anyone. Not even family.

Mr. Garrison grinned, and Liz didn't try to stop her lip from quivering. She would miss his smile, his laugh, his advice. He was one of only two people she'd always wished belonged to her by something as strong as blood. Right now, she wanted a lifeline stretching between them so she'd never lose him.

"I'm an old man, and there's a lot you don't know about me."

She huffed, and another tear ran down her cheek. He was right, but she thought she knew more about him than most people knew about their next-door neighbors. She'd done more than live in the house beside his for the last eighteen years. She'd bonded with him.

"I have business partners in Dallas. People I trust. They're helping me locate someone you can live with."

It was real. She was moving... tonight. Liz had never been more than twenty-five miles outside of the small town of Carson, Georgia, but she was moving to Dallas indefinitely, tonight.

"Listen here, Liz."

She lifted her chin to meet his demand. Liz had never balked at obeying Mr. Garrison. He'd never yelled at her or hit her like her dad.

"Sheriff Tubbs is trustworthy too. You'll be safe with him."

Her eyes were tingling now. Too many tears and not enough sleep. "How do you have business partners that you've never mentioned before?" Her words were soft yet questioning. "You think we can trust them?"

Mr. Garrison shook his head and rubbed a hand over his sparse, white beard. "I lived a full life before you came along, Lizzy. They're not in the business of puttin' up young girls in safe homes, that's for sure. But they're people who have enough money to buy loyalty and silence. If we don't do this, the marshals will soon."

She noticed that he hadn't answered her question, but she let it slide. "What about Ian?"

Liz knew what Mr. Garrison would say, and she braced herself for the impact. The blow that would kick the life out of what was left of her hope.

It was the spring holiday, and Ian was on vacation with his family on the Gulf Coast. He wouldn't be back for another three days. Normally, Ian would have opted to stay behind, but his mom had wanted one last family vacation together before he joined the marines after graduation. His family traveled often, but Liz knew Ian never tagged along because he was reluctant to leave her.

Right now, her heart was torn. The selfish part of her, the part that was a creature of habit and longed for the comfort only her best friend could give her, wished he was here. But the selfless part of her heart, the part that cared about Ian more than any other person in the world, was glad he wasn't. It made leaving him a little easier.

Mr. Garrison tapped the bottom of his cane on the linoleum floor. "That's up to you. I can fill him in when he gets back if that's what you want. He'll want to be with you, and I can arrange to get him there."

Liz covered her face with her hands and cried fresh tears. Of course, Ian would come for her. He wouldn't finish high school. He wouldn't honor his commitment to the marines. He would spend his life beside her, running from an invisible enemy. He couldn't do that. Not for her. It was time for her to let Ian go and let him live his life without the burden of protecting her.

They weren't even in a relationship. They were just friends, and Ian deserved a chance to meet someone and have a normal life.

That's why she couldn't tell him.

Ian was the one who always came to her rescue, but even he couldn't save her now.

"No." She wiped her face again. "He can't. You can't."

Mr. Garrison's eyes turned glassy as he nodded. He pulled a folded handkerchief from his back pocket and wiped his nose. "The people I send for you will protect you. I'll send money and a new phone number where you can reach me. We can't use our phones anymore. The McCalls aren't affluent, but they won't take this sittin' down. We know that much."

Liz nodded and looked out the window of Mr. Garrison's kitchen. She could see Ian's house dimly lit by the midnight streetlights. She'd never speak to Ian Hart again.

Mr. Garrison reached out his thick, wrinkled hand and laid it atop hers. "I'm proud of you, sweetheart. You'll do fine on your own. You might even do better when you get outta here. There are better things in the world than what you've known here."

Liz bit her lip and stifled the urge to reject his words. There wasn't anything out there that could compare to Ian or the way she felt about him.

Her girlish heart had accepted him, her pre-teen heart had clung to him, and her eighteen-year-old heart had loved him with every fiber of her being. He just didn't know it.

Sheriff Tubbs walked back into the kitchen and sighed. "Everything is set." He turned to Liz, and his look of pity almost sent her sobbing again. "Your new name is Sara Williams. You'll have proper documentation later this week." He turned to Mr. Garrison. "The plane is waiting at the Cherokee County airstrip."

Panic gripped Liz's chest as she turned back to her neighbor. "What? I'm Sara now? And I'm flying?" She'd never even been close to an airplane before, and she didn't know what to expect.

"Don't worry. Sara is a common name, and Sheriff Tubbs is flying with you. His brother is a pilot and agreed to take you."

Liz was crying again. She wasn't sure if the on-and-off waterworks would stop anytime soon.

Mr. Garrison stood and pulled her to her feet and hugged her close. He smelled like cigar smoke and butterscotch, his favorite candy.

"Come on, sweetheart. It's not the end. I think it's your beginning. I wish you could stay, but I care about you too much to risk your life because I love you." Mr. Garrison might have been a grumpy old man to most people, but his heart had always been soft for Liz.

She let him lead her outside, one hand holding hers and the other on his cane. When she stood beside Sheriff Tubbs' undercover car, she risked one more look at Ian's family home. It had been the safest place she'd known, and now she was expected to leave it.

"I can tell him. It's up to you," Mr. Garrison reminded her.

"No, it's better this way." She believed her words, but another part of her was screaming inside. Ian would never forgive her.

Liz felt nothing for her own home, which sat dark and dilapidated on the other side of Mr. Garrison's yard. It didn't deserve a parting glance. Those walls had seen too much and done nothing to protect her.

Now was not the time to trip on her heart. She may never see Ian again, but Mr. Garrison's words rang in her head. Maybe this wasn't the end for her. She'd always wanted to get away from home, but her dreams of running away had always included Ian at her side—two friends off to find some adventure outside of Carson.

How funny to think that when it came time to get out of Dodge, she'd be sneaking away in the night without him.

She swallowed her tears and let her hand slip from

Mr. Garrison's grip. Once she was in the car, he closed the door and gave her a strained smile. He was trying to hold himself together for her sake, but she knew his heart. She wasn't sure she'd have made it eighteen years without the old man looking after her.

Sheriff Tubbs slipped into the driver's seat and turned to give her a nod. "You're gonna be okay. You're better off gettin' away from this place."

She knew his words were true, but she didn't have to like them.

She focused on her hands in her lap, wringing them ceaselessly as the car moved away from her home. Not her house, but Ian.

He'd thank her one day. He'd see that this was for the best.

She, however, might not fare so well. Right now, she was holding on and letting go.

Sara

TWELVE YEARS LATER

Sara slowed her steps as she neared Andrew Spiker's office. The Spiker Law Firm was small but conveniently located adjacent to the Cherokee County Courthouse in downtown Carson. Andrew was an old high school friend, and it seemed he was doing well for himself.

Sara jammed the pad of her thumb into the sharp edges of her front teeth. The small bite of pain distracted her from the gnawing worry she felt in her middle.

She could've refused to come, but curiosity killed the cat. She was only human, and she couldn't live the rest of her life without knowing why Mr. Garrison had asked her to come back here. Enough years had passed that any threat to her life had grown dormant but not died. The men she hid from had been securely locked up or scattered to the four winds for over a decade, and that should've been a comfort to her.

The door was heavy, but she pushed her way into the office where a familiar face awaited her.

Tracy Sawyer sucked in an excited breath and stood from where she'd been clicking away on a keyboard behind the front desk.

Opening her arms for a hug, Tracy exclaimed, "Liz!"

before shrinking back and covering her mouth with both hands. "I mean—"

"It's fine," Sara whispered as she positioned her purse strap higher onto her shoulder. "Happens all the time."

That was a lie, but Sara was sure it would soon become one of those mishaps that did in fact happen all the time now that she was back in Carson where everyone knew her as Liz Jennings instead of Sara Williams.

The look of embarrassment didn't fade from Tracy's face. "I'm just so sorry. I don't know what I was thinking." She rung her hands and forced a smile. "I've been so excited to see you since Andrew told me the situation. I had no idea! I'd always heard you went to live with your grandparents in Idaho."

So, that was the story that Mr. Garrison and the sheriff had spun. It was plausible. She'd give them that. Sara had gone through school with both Tracy and Andrew, and it was nice to see that they were still in town and doing okay.

The excitement of Tracy's greeting had diminished, and she forgot about her intended hug. "Can I get you something to drink?"

"I'm fine, but thanks."

Tracy tilted her chin toward the hallway. "This way." She stepped to the side and walked slowly, turning her body to continue talking face-to-face. "I didn't believe it when Drew told me. What an awful story! But you seem like you're doin' just fine now. You look great."

Sara *felt* great... most days. Getting away from Carson had been good for her. At least, that's what she told herself when she'd been able to go to college and get a graduate-level degree—something completely unheard of when she'd been growing up in Georgia.

"Thanks. You do too. It's been a while. How are you?"

Sara suddenly felt at a disadvantage that someone she hadn't spoken to in over a decade knew so much about her. After spending years keeping secrets, she thought it would feel nice to have someone finally know the truth. Instead, she felt only worry. She hoped Tracy could be trusted not to spill what she knew.

"I'm married now. We have two kids. Joey is seven, and Katie is five. Oh, and we have a cat named Rolo. We live out in Glenbrook. My husband, Ken, is an accountant with Lipscom and Burke."

Sara wanted to be happy for Tracy, but her mind only wondered how much of what the receptionist heard at work was confided to her husband in the evenings.

"It sounds like you're doing well." Sara's words were lifeless as her anxiety mounted.

Tracy stopped in front of a door and placed her hand on the knob. "I am. Life is good." Tracy's true smile had returned, but soon faded as she leaned toward Sara and whispered, "Someone else is in there. Fair warning. I don't know what terms y'all are on these days, but... Well, I'm only sayin' something because there are so few people on Ian's good side."

Sara's breathing halted at the name. She'd known there was a possibility she'd see Ian while she was here, but she wasn't ready. She wasn't sure she would ever be ready to see him again.

Nodding, Sara swallowed the worry that clogged her throat. "Thanks, Tracy."

"No problem. What are friends for?"

Sara wasn't sure she would've labeled Tracy her friend back in high school. She'd been more like an acquaintance, but Sara had certainly been closer to Tracy than most anyone she'd met since leaving Carson.

Tracy opened the door to a conference room housing a long table surrounded by chairs, but the only thing Sara could see was the man sitting at the table.

A look of surprised recognition washed over Ian's face, and for a moment, she saw her best friend. Just as quickly as it had arrived, the innocent look was gone, replaced by a scowl.

She knew it well—that intimidating look that had sent so many running after they'd picked on her or caused her a second's grief when she was younger.

The boy Sara used to know was now a man. His features were much the same yet hardened and strikingly handsome. As if her heart needed another reason to be drawn to him. She'd already lost herself to him years ago. It was easy to fall for him when she knew the heart he hid behind the scowl.

Maybe it was because she associated that piercing stare with his loyalty to her. That face had always meant someone had hurt her, done her wrong, or undervalued her, and that Ian was on a mission to right their wrongs.

Now, that scowl was directed at her, and she didn't like it, even if she deserved it. She felt a tugging notion in the recesses of her mind that said she should tread lightly. Ian should've been intimidating, after all, but she'd been a firsthand witness to his tenderness before.

There were darker evils in this world worth fearing.

Sara had lived most of her life on the protected side of Ian's rage. She wondered how far his anger would take him now that she was back, standing before him wearing the secrets she'd kept from him.

Ian carefully stood to his full height, and she restrained her surprise. He'd always been tall, but he towered above her in the small conference room.

Neither of them broke the silence that flooded the room since Tracy closed them in together. She had rolled this moment over in her mind thousands of times, but she was paralyzed when faced with the reality. She wondered if Ian felt the same or if he simply had nothing to say to her.

Before Sara gathered up the nerve to either speak or

sit, the door opened, and Andrew stormed into the room as if he hadn't shattered a fragile tension between two broken strangers.

"Thanks for coming. I'll try to make this quick so you can get back to it." Andrew sat in the chair at the head of the table and opened a folder. "It's good to see you both. Everything going good for you?"

Andrew hadn't directed the question at either of them, but Ian kept his intense gaze locked on her as he answered. "Yep."

Sara tried to slide into the seat beside Andrew and directly across from Ian without disturbing the ceasefire. "Yeah, I'm good. You?"

"Oh, yeah." Andrew flipped through the stack of papers until he found the one he was looking for. "Been married for a few years now. Kids are great."

Andrew had always been a studious kid in school. It was nice to see that he'd settled into a profession where he could help people. He'd always been kind to her before she left.

Sara silently wished that Ian would've really answered the question. She ached to know something, anything, about him.

"Let's get started. I'm really sorry about Mr. Garrison's passing. We worked together quite a bit in his last few years, and I know why the two of you took to him so well. He was a good man."

Sara promised herself she wouldn't cry, but hearing Andrew talk about her old friend had her breath coming in shallow pants. This would be harder than she'd expected. Apparently, she hadn't exhausted her tears after Andrew's phone call two days ago.

"What was it?" Sara's question was almost a whisper. The obituary had been short and lacking any telling information, and she'd been so upset when Andrew called with the news that she hadn't asked. There wouldn't even be a memorial service. Mr. Garrison had been a private man, and he'd never given into the notion that he should succumb to pleasantries for the sake of tradition.

"Cancer," Andrew answered. "He found out early enough that he could make arrangements, but not early enough to beat it."

Sara dipped her chin because she knew the tears were right below the surface. Why hadn't Mr. Garrison told her about it? She'd have done anything in her power to be there for him. The reminder that her friend had died alone hit her like a fresh branding iron.

"You probably know that he left most of his assets to the two of you. There were a few others named, but their shares were minimal compared to yours."

Sara's curiosity piqued again. She'd been wondering for days what Mr. Garrison could've possibly left her. He'd already spent so much on her. From relocating her, to security, to paying for her college education in full, Mr. Garrison had spent a fortune on her in the last decade.

Of course, she'd offered to pay him back when she finally landed a job, but he wouldn't accept a cent from her. He'd kept the source of his money a secret from her the whole time. How had he been able to send her such large amounts of money so often?

"Mr. Garrison had detailed instructions for how I'm supposed to tell you about everything. First, he wanted me to tell you both that he's proud of you. You were both given enormous gifts, and neither of you squandered it. Apparently, you both wanted to know how he came into his fortune, and he wanted me to tell you that, in his early years, he was the co-owner of the top uniform production company in the country. Garrison Corp. supplied the United States Armed Forces with uniforms, as well as many law enforcement and firefighter agencies. Needless to say, Mr. Garrison had retained the title of billionaire for over half his life."

"What?" Sara gasped in disbelief. "A billionaire? What was he doing living on Dover Lane?"

Mr. Garrison had lived in the modest house between hers and Ian's since before she was born. Mr. Garrison could've lived anywhere he pleased. Why the secluded Dover Lane in Carson, Georgia?

Andrew shrugged. "Even I don't know the answer to that. He said he had his reasons, but he also said he wanted you to know so that you'd stop worrying about paying him back. He didn't have any heirs, so he considered the two of you his own."

Sara risked a glance at Ian to find his intimidating glare still locked on her. She wasn't sure he was breathing. He could've passed for a statue.

"The terms," Andrew began. "Ian, you'll receive an annual stipend to be used to further your business ventures. Mr. Garrison was pleased with the progress you'd made with the hardware store, and he wanted to make sure the business continued to prosper."

Finally, she saw Ian draw in and release a deep breath as if hearing his name had jolted him out of his paralysis.

"And for you, Sara—"

"Sara?" Ian asked. "Who is Sara?"

Anger rolled off Ian in waves, and Sara couldn't do more than continue to breathe.

"Liz's name is Sara now," Andrew explained. "It was important that we used her legal name for probate purposes so she'd be able to claim the money legally."

Ian sat up straighter. "I mean, why is her name Sara now?" He wasn't even speaking to her. She might as well have been invisible.

Andrew's gaze flicked to hers when she didn't answer. "I haven't been given permission to disclose that information."

Ian sat back in his chair and narrowed his gaze at her. "Still the last to know. Fine."

She'd expected his wrath, but feeling it this close was hard to stomach.

Ian was a fire, always burning hot enough to keep everyone around him at a distance. It seemed he'd only grown more destructive in the years they'd been apart.

She understood his pain, and she welcomed his anger. His rage was powerful, but her guilt was worse.

When Andrew was satisfied that Ian wouldn't fly off the deep end, he continued. "Um, Sara, you are set to inherit one billion dollars—"

"What?" she interrupted and looked to Ian to gauge his reaction. Not so much as a tic passed his features, and she wondered how much he'd known about Mr. Garrison before today.

Andrew pressed on. "Mr. Garrison has included in his notes that he's aware of your dream, and he's sorry he isn't around to see you fulfill it."

Sara had harbored a bleeding heart for battered women and children her whole life. After the years she'd spent with her dad, her greatest wish had always been to help others. That's why she'd become a youth counselor. But she often volunteered at a home for women and children, and Mr. Garrison had known.

"The sum of this inheritance is to be paid to you in full upon the completion of Mr. Garrison's stipulation."

Sara couldn't form the words to ask what that might be. All she could think about was how many people she could save with one billion dollars.

Andrew went on. "Mr. Garrison is in possession of a plot of twenty acres just east of Carson. The two of you are to renovate the home, together, before any money will be distributed to either of you."

Andrew looked up and swiveled his gaze between Sara and Ian. "He also said that he knew there was a chance that one or both of you would decline the inheritance. He wanted me to stress to you that the most important part of his inheritance is that the two of you work together on this house. He said it was time for you to put the past behind you and give the future a chance."

Sara knew better than to trust the idea of a future. She'd spent too many years looking over her shoulder, waiting for the end to find her.

She looked up and her gaze met Ian's. What kind of chance did she have of a future with the frown staring back at her? It wouldn't be easy to trust the one person who didn't trust her in return.

Ian

Ian set his jaw tight to restrain his protest. If he had any control over his own choices right now, he'd walk out of this room and never look back.

At least, that's what he should do. But he'd made a promise years ago that he intended to keep. Granted, he hadn't known what he was promising at the time. Now that it was time to settle up, Ian wanted to curse the old man.

He couldn't hear half of what Andrew was saying. Seeing Liz again had captivated his attention.

Correction, *Sara*.

She looked amazing. Gorgeous, poised, and confident. She looked like she had life wrapped around her finger.

She'd managed fine without him. Why did it hurt to see her doing so well? Probably because she didn't need him as much as he'd needed her. He had wanted to pave the way for her to chase all her dreams, and it looked as if she'd managed just fine without him.

He'd recognized Liz the moment she'd walked through the doorway, but he hadn't expected her to be such a knockout. He'd always been attracted to Liz, and the things he felt for her extended beyond the physical.

Still, it was hard to imagine she could be more beautiful than the last time he saw her.

Her brown hair was longer, and it hung in soft waves. Her facial features were more striking and alluring. Those lips he'd always dreamt of kissing were fuller, and her eyes were perfectly accentuated by subtle makeup. He'd never seen her wearing makeup or with styled hair before. Not to mention her clothes. She wore a billowing navy blouse and tight white pants, as if she belonged at a country club luncheon.

Where was Liz?

He wanted to scream, and he wanted to run to her. There'd been a time when being around Liz had been as common as eating breakfast, lunch, and dinner. Why did she still confuse him after all this time? His sweet Liz was finally here, right in front of him, but he'd never felt so far away from her.

Ian barely heard Andrew as he told them Mr. Garrison's plea that they give the future a chance. Ian wanted to scoff. Their future had died when she left without him. He was still processing the fact that not only had Mr. Garrison known where Liz was all along, but he'd been in deep contact with her. How many times had Ian asked the old man if he knew? Each time, his neighbor and friend had lied.

The betrayal hurt. Almost as bad as Liz—no, *Sara's* betrayal. Certainly more than Julie's deceit. Apparently, Ian didn't incite loyalty in anyone he knew and trusted.

Even Andrew had known where she was. Why hadn't Liz trusted Ian to know?

Better yet, why hadn't she trusted him with her safety or her heart? Hadn't he proven time and time again that he'd do anything for her?

"Ian?" Andrew asked.

Ian turned to the attorney and tilted his head. What was Andrew asking?

"Do you agree to uphold the terms of the inheritance?" Andrew repeated.

Ian looked at Liz again. He'd barely been able to take his eyes from her. "Yeah. I'll do it." Whatever it might be. He wasn't sure what all he was agreeing to, but he'd get Andrew to catch him up later.

"Good. I have instructions and letters for both of you. Here's the address to the property. Sara, you've been instructed to remain on the property at all times."

She nodded, as if she'd expected the stipulation.

"Ian, you're to retrieve any supplies needed for the renovation, as well as any supplies and groceries Sara may need during her stay. You're not allowed to tell anyone what you're doing or where you go." Andrew turned his full attention on Ian. "This is the biggest secret you'll ever be asked to keep."

Ian scoffed. "More secrets."

Andrew ignored Ian's ire and continued. "You're only allowed to seek assistance from two outsiders. You can consult Brian Matthews for construction assistance and Jake Sims for security or protection."

"Do they know about this?" Ian asked.

Andrew nodded. "They've been made aware of the possibility that their assistance may be needed and why, but they should only be called on when you're unable to help. Your main job is to protect Sara and tell no one."

"I don't even know what I would be telling!" Ian exclaimed, holding his palms up in confusion. Years ago, he hadn't even been asked to protect her. He'd done it readily without hesitation. Now, he was being manipulated into it. That old man knew that Ian would do anything for Liz, and if it meant she got the money she needed to fulfill some dream, he couldn't say no. He rubbed his hands hard over the short, coarse hair on his head. He needed to get out of here.

Andrew's look of pity had Ian itching to hit something. His punching bag would take a beating tonight.

"It's better this way," Andrew chided. "Sara, you'll report to the house in the morning. Stay out of sight until then. Ian, you're to stock the house with things that Sara may need to live there. I've arranged for the electricity, water, and gas to be turned on."

Andrew slid them each a bronze key and a note. When neither of them reached for the items, Andrew cleared his throat. "I guess that's all. I'll be in touch with both of you, so... I guess it was good to see you."

The attorney stood, and Liz followed. Ian took his time, allowing both of them to exit before grabbing the note and key into one hand. He wasn't eager to read the letter. He'd had enough of the old man's orders for one day.

When Ian stepped into the hallway, the high, sinister voice of Ms. Miller had his fists clenching.

"My appointment was for 2:00. It's fifteen after!"

Ms. Miller's tirade ceased when she spotted Liz emerging from the hallway toward the exit.

Liz, or Sara rather, ducked her head enough that her hair fell in a sheet between her and Ms. Miller as her stride quickened toward the door fast enough that the town busybody might not have recognized her.

Ian caught up to Liz just as she turned the corner and rounded on him. Worry covered her face like a mask as a crease formed between her brows.

"Is Ms. Miller still a gossip like she used to be?" Liz asked.

Ian clenched his jaw before snapping, "Still the same. Doesn't keep secrets."

A look of sadness washed over Liz's face as she whispered, "I'm not trying to keep secrets."

Ian stepped closer to her. If she wasn't trying to keep secrets, then what exactly did she call the last twelve years? "I'd like to know what changed."

And so much more, but first things first. "One minute, you told me everything, and I knew everything about you. The next, you're gone!" Ian flung his arms out at his sides. "Not one response to my texts or calls. Not even to let me know you were alive."

He watched Liz's throat ripple as she swallowed before tucking her chin. Then he went on. "I won't sit here and explain what you did to me. You know. Whatever happened to you, I could've been there beside you." Ian shoved a finger at his chest to release a tiny bit of frustration.

Liz sighed. "I wish you knew."

"Yeah, that makes two of us. I'll see you tomorrow."

Ian turned and walked back to his truck before he did something stupid, like pull her into his arms.

Ian

The truck door slammed, locking Ian inside the silent cab. He missed his old truck. The door had creaked and protested with the scrape of metal on metal each time he'd taken out his frustrations on it. His new, luxury pickup was a joke.

Ian shoved the gear into reverse and peeled out of the parking spot without hesitation.

The stop sign not twenty feet from where he'd parked really took the heat out of his storm-and-run, but he used the pause to call his friend, Jake. The one he'd now refer to as the Keeper of Secrets.

Jake's voice pounded through the speakers of Ian's truck after the first ring. Deputy Jake Sims was always on alert.

"What's up?"

"Oh, nothing. I've just been informed that I'm the first line of defense for a ghost. Anything you wanna tell me about Liz Jennings, brother? Or should I say Sara Williams?"

There was a pause on the line before Jake stammered, "Um, I..."

"Save it," Ian barked. "Meet me at the hardware store."

"Now?" Jake asked.

"Now."

"Yes, sir." Jake liked to keep the peace, and he'd likely been waiting for this reckoning.

Ian disconnected the call and decided against giving Brian a warning. His friend would be at the hardware store the two of them co-owned.

Ian twisted the steering wheel in his hands so hard that the sensation felt like rope burn. Good. He deserved the pain.

He'd spent years destroying everything meaningful in his life, afraid to hope that something good could touch him. That was his punishment for not being good enough to her—for being a monster to everyone since she'd left.

Now, it was too much to hope that he could fall back into the arms of grace. There'd been a Liz-sized hole missing from his heart for too long, and the loss had rotted his insides. He'd taped up the wound a long time ago, but the festering had poisoned everything in its wake.

There were boxes—more like metal safes—in his brain where the memories of his Liz stayed. Locked up where they couldn't hurt him anymore.

He wasn't ready for them to come out. He wasn't ready to remember, but seeing her, being close enough to touch her, made him want more.

Ian pulled into his designated parking spot behind the hardware store and shifted into park. Along with the key, the note Andrew had given him sat crumpled in the passenger seat beside him. Ian couldn't read it now. He had some friends who owed him answers.

Ian stormed in through the back door and caught sight of Brian talking to Lindsey in the hallway by the offices.

"You." Ian pointed to Brian. "My office. Now." Ian's tone was sharp, but his friend didn't flinch.

Brian turned to their bookkeeper, Lindsey, and shrugged. "Boss man calls."

Ian made his way behind the desk and sat down, while Brian took his time sauntering in and closing the door behind him.

"You summoned me?" Brian quipped.

"How long have you known about Liz?" No sense in beating around the bush.

Brian had the sense to look shocked before moving to sit in the chair that faced Ian's desk. "Oh, is that happening?"

"Is *what* happening?" Ian questioned.

"Well, Mr. Garrison gave me a rundown years ago about some plans he made. I guess this means the old man passed." Brian's easy smile had faded completely. "I hadn't realized."

"So, you knew about this years ago? And you didn't tell me!"

Brian sat up straighter. "What was I supposed to do? I trust the old man, and he's smarter than all of us put together. If he'd wanted to bring Liz back sooner, he would've done it." Brian's features became serious, and he shoved a finger at Ian. "But you're just now starting to get your act together. Do you blame him for keeping her away?"

Ian knew the truth in his friend's words, but that didn't make them easier to swallow. "You all lied to me. About *her* of all things."

"You were desperate... for a long time. Desperation makes people do stupid things. Maybe you weren't what was best for her."

Ian questioned Brian's intelligence sometimes. It wasn't smart to poke the bear. Instead of saying so, Ian kept quiet and focused on controlling his anger, the emotion that ruled him. *Breathe in. Breathe out.*

Brian leaned forward, propping his arms on the desk and linking his fingers. "This is your chance. The one you've waited a long time for. Don't screw it up because you don't know how to be anything but miserable."

Ian growled through gritted teeth. "It isn't that simple."

"Isn't it?" Brian asked. "Liz needs you, and I know you'll step up and protect her, but she needs you to be her friend again too. She needs you to listen."

"She hasn't told me anything!"

"She will," Brian assured.

The door opened, and Jake stepped in wearing his tan deputy uniform. "Hey, what'd I miss?"

Brian turned to look at Jake but didn't answer.

Ian hung his head in his hands and sighed. The fire had gone out of him. Railing at his friends was only misdirecting his anger.

"Nothing," Ian said. "I'm just frustrated that everyone knew where Liz was except me. By the way, her name is Sara Williams now. That's taking me a minute to get used to."

Brian perked up. "To be fair, we didn't know where she was. Only that she was meant to come back one day, and that the two of you might need our help."

Jake nodded. "It's the truth, man. We didn't want to keep anything from you, but after Liz left, you weren't in the best state of mind. Then you were off with the marines, and we thought that would do you some good —to get to do what you always wanted to do. Then you were discharged and Julie did her number on you, and you were worse. Liz didn't need that. I mean Sara. She needed stability."

Ian pinched the bridge of his nose. "I get it. I don't deserve her. Can we maybe skip this part?"

"No." Jake stepped closer to the desk. "It's not that you didn't deserve her. It's that you don't understand what she went through, and you can't until you give her a chance to realize that you're still the same person you were before—the one she trusted with everything."

Brian nodded and jerked his thumb over his shoulder toward Jake. "Right. What he said."

"Fine." Ian pulled the small note from his pocket with the address that Andrew had given him typed on it. "Here's where she's staying and where I'll be if I need anything from the two of you. Memorize it. I'm burning this when I leave here."

Brian took the note, read it, and passed it to Jake.

Ian powered on his computer. "Now get out. I have work to do."

Brian saluted him, and Jake said nothing as they stepped out of the office.

Ian's anger continued to boil right below the surface, but he needed to focus on work and take his mind off Liz.

He knew what his friends had said was true. His anger had distanced him from everyone, but it was hard to put aside years of hurt to let Liz come to him at her own pace. He wanted answers, and he wanted them twelve years ago.

He sucked in a deep breath through his nose as the spreadsheet filled the screen in front of him. Patience wasn't his strong suit, and Liz's return had him all shook up.

Liz had kept her secrets, and now, so had his friends and his neighbor. It was too much for one day.

Tomorrow, he would have to see her again, and he wasn't sure he was ready.

Sara

S ara snuck out of her room at Bernard's Hotel
before sunrise. She wasn't always so cautious, but
being back in the place where her lifelong game
of hide-and-seek started made her want to take advantage of the cover of darkness to leave the hotel.

She'd packed light and hadn't left much of anything
in her apartment in Memphis. She'd moved more than
half a dozen times since leaving Carson, and this move
was proving to be simple so far. Not as simple as that
first move, but two suitcases now held everything she
owned.

Following the GPS on her phone, she drove beyond
the town's limits and slowed as she turned onto the last
drive her navigation device recognized. It was a gravel
road almost completely covered by trees, and there
wasn't a house in sight.

Sara checked her mirrors and kept her gaze darting
to one side and the other. No one was around, but she'd
been living a life of caution for too long to give it
up now.

A dirt road with a mailbox at the end caught her attention. It was the only sign of life she'd seen in a mile.
Sure enough, the numbers on the box read 5304, the
address Andrew had given her.

She turned her Camry into the drive and crept up the washed-out, curvy road. What was Mr. Garrison doing with a house way out here? The only answer that came to her mind was that he'd bought it for her—with a purpose.

Sara tried not to think about Mr. Garrison's goal in his detailed inheritance scheme. She could've said no. She didn't *need* the money, but she knew others did. He'd known she'd use the money to save anyone she could from the childhood she'd suffered.

The trees that covered the drive opened to a clearing small enough that the sun barely touched it. A one-level house with a gray roof and dirty white walls that almost touched the trees on three sides filled the area. The red dirt and gravel road ended in front of the house and fanned out to form what was meant to be extra parking.

No front porch. No garage. Just a square house that had been here for so long that it almost blended into the woods and earth that surrounded it. It was old, but the bones must be good to still be standing after all these years.

The sound of her car door slamming pierced the silence of the forest. She didn't know what time Ian would be arriving, but she wanted to get inside and assess the project they'd be working on.

Before she'd finished pulling her bags from the trunk of the car, a silver pickup truck made its way through the trees and parked beside her car.

A GMC Denali. Ian must be doing well for himself.

He stepped out of the truck, and she was surprised again by his height. He towered above her small car.

While she stood admiring him, Ian walked right up to her, and her heart pounded harder with each step he took toward her.

Without hesitating, he grabbed the bag in the trunk with one hand and hoisted it out as if it weighed as much as her purse. He pointed to the handle of the other bag that she gripped in her hand, and she released it.

With both bags in tow, he made his way toward the door on the side of the house.

Gaining her wits, she rushed to beat him there. She fumbled in the back pocket of her jeans and produced the key just as he made it to the door.

She unlocked it and shoved it open. Ian lifted his chin, indicating that she should enter first. Stepping into the kitchen, she moved out of the doorway so he could bring the bags in.

They both stopped, and Ian growled through gritted teeth, "If he wasn't already dead—"

"Stop it," Sara chided. "Surely, he didn't know this place was..."

Ian gave her a stern look that said he didn't believe her.

"Okay, it's a dump," Sara conceded.

"That's generous."

The linoleum floors were buckling. The counter-tops were cracked. Wallpaper had once hung on the walls, but some of the strips had wilted and curled off. The place must've been vacant for years.

Sara took a deep breath, resigned to the enormous task ahead of them. "Let's just get to work."

The last few days had been one big blow after the other. She was back in the place where she'd grown up, the place she'd never thought she'd return to. To top it all off, she was confined to a small space with Ian Hart, the man she'd never dared hope to see again.

It felt as if she'd been missing a part of herself. The part that should've been with her best friend for the last decade.

She was going to be living in the place where she'd last known love. She would never know if Ian had felt the same way about her all those years ago, but *she'd* felt it, and that made it real.

Ian carried the bags into the adjoining room, and she reminded herself that she'd made a decision back then that she couldn't take back. She'd chosen to leave him behind, and she still had to live with her decision.

Sara stepped to the sink and turned the water on. It flowed brown for a few minutes before clearing. She shut it off and moved to the refrigerator and opened it to see if it worked.

It did, but the musty smell had her gagging. She hoped Ian had brought cleaning supplies.

As if he'd been summoned by her thoughts, the rhythmic thud of Ian's footsteps pounded down the hallway. He stepped back into the kitchen, and she scoured her thoughts for something to say. There was so much to do, and the long list overwhelmed her.

"I put the bags in one of the bedrooms. If one of the two was bigger than the other, I couldn't tell." He motioned toward the door. "The supplies are in the truck."

She pointed into the open refrigerator she stood in front of. "Did you get cleaning supplies?"

"Yep. I got most everything except fridge items. I wanted to make sure the power was really on first."

He was walking out the door, so she followed him.

Ian called over his shoulder as she followed him. "There's furniture in the bedroom, but I just realized you'll need sheets and blankets. I'll get those this afternoon."

"Thanks. And thank you for doing all this. I know you have a life, and this is... disrupting." She'd lied to avoid interrupting his life all those years ago, but none of that mattered now.

Ian didn't turn to her as he grabbed about twenty grocery bags in both hands. "It's fine."

A flicker of disappointment moved through her, but she couldn't really fault him for being short with her. There was a lot she hadn't told him about her own life, so she couldn't expect him to spill his guts.

They made trips from the truck to the kitchen bringing in the bags. Ian really had gotten most everything she would need, and she made a quick list of a few missing items.

"I'll give you cash for this before you leave," Sara said as she scribbled on the notepad Ian had brought.

"No need. Mr. Garrison set up an account for house-related expenses."

Sara looked up from the notepad. "He really thought this through."

Ian didn't look up from the bags he was unloading. "I hope it was worth it."

She didn't know how to respond to that, so she kept quiet as they unloaded the bags. The hours stretched on, and the silence dominated the rest of the day as they tended to separate tasks. They didn't even speak through a hasty lunch of sandwiches she'd prepared for them beyond his thanks.

Around 4:00 in the evening, Ian grabbed the list she'd made and left, locking the door behind him. He returned with dinner, more bulging bags, and a new mattress for the bed. She hadn't even thought of the bed she'd be sleeping in tonight. She helped him unload the mattress and the bags again... in silence.

When night had fallen completely, Ian stepped into the bathroom where she was cleaning the tub.

"I'll be back in the morning. I'll bring breakfast."

She nodded, unsure if she could trust her voice not to break if she spoke. Being in the house with Ian all day without speaking was breaking her heart, and her mood had been sinking faster by the minute.

When Ian was gone, Sara located all the toiletries she'd need for a shower and cried while the scalding water washed away the smell of bleach that clung to her skin.

She fell into the new mattress and fought memory-driven dreams. Flashes of the years she and Ian had grown up together.

Liz was young, no more than ten. She held a flashlight in her dark bedroom over a letter from her grandmother. Her mom's mom. Liz's mom hadn't cared about her enough to stick around, but she knew her grandma loved her because she wrote her letters. Her mom's folks had sent her money a few times, but her dad didn't let her keep it. He always took it before she got the mail. Liz only knew about it because her grandma wrote about it in the letters.

Her dad's folks didn't love Liz at all. Daddy came from a long line of sinners. Not that Liz hadn't too, but at least she didn't like it. Her daddy didn't know the difference between good and bad. She wasn't sure if he'd ever heard about the golden rule, but he sure didn't follow it. She only knew about it because they talked about it in Sunday School when she went with Ian.

The words on the page blurred as she thought about her daddy. Why didn't he do anything for himself? Liz made food sometimes when she got hungry and could find something in the kitchen, and she always made enough for him too. She'd learned how to wash their clothes and the dishes. She changed his sheets and vacuumed.

Daddy never did anything. All he cared about was fighting roosters at the Ritter Farm in Bradford.

Liz swallowed hard. Maybe Daddy was still mad at her. He'd told her she was a mistake—a girl that should'a been a boy. Then he'd made her wish she would have ducked sooner because he was mad, and Liz still wasn't a boy.

Liz heard shuffling at the front door and lifted her head to listen. When the banging against the door got louder, she wiped the tears off her face and scooted toward the window. That wasn't Daddy, and she couldn't think of anything else to do but run.

Liz pushed the heavy window up and scooted out into the dark night. She ran across Mr. Garrison's backyard in her bare feet. The damp grass had numbed her soles by the time she'd tapped her knuckles against Ian's bedroom window.

Ian pushed the curtains to the side and lifted the window as soon as he saw her. "Liz, what's wrong?"

"Can I come in? Daddy isn't home, and I think someone's trying to get in." Her words shook, and she knew it was from fear, not cold.

"Get in here." He helped her climb into the room and pulled her into a hug as soon as she stood upright.

"Good grief, Liz. You're freezing. Here, get in." He pointed to the rumpled covers piled atop his bed. "I'll tell Mom you're here, and she'll get you something hot to eat and call the cops."

"No." She was whispering and screaming at the same time. Her teeth were chattering, but she fought to keep her voice steady. "I'm okay. I just needed to get outta there. Don't call the cops. They'll take me away from him, and..."

And you. That's what she hadn't been able to say. She endured the slaps and her dad's harsh words because she didn't want to go anywhere. She liked being close to her best friend more than she hated being hit on.

Ian stood in the middle of the dark room, debating.

"Please," she pleaded. "I won't stay long. I just got scared."

Ian's eternal scowl had already begun to form at the early age of ten. "You can stay as long as you want. Just get in the bed. I can't stand it that you're cold."

Ian had slept in a pile of blankets on the floor. Liz had fallen into the best sleep of her life that night and woken up before sunrise. She snuck out before Ian's parents woke up, and that was the beginning. Whenever her dad hit her, or she knew he'd had too much to drink and feared he'd storm into her room and remind her that she was a burden, she'd run to Ian.

He'd open the window for her and be waiting with open arms. That was her home. The place where someone cared about her. The place where someone was waiting to hold her when her heart couldn't take another beating. Where she felt safe and free.

He learned early that she didn't always like talking about whatever darkness she was running from, and they made up their own sign language. He'd lie on the floor beside the bed, and she'd let her arm dangle off the side. The only time their skin met was when he tapped her hand. Three taps meant "Are you all right?" One tap for yes and two taps for no.

She always tapped once. She really was okay, as long as she was with Ian. Any other time, there was no one around to tap three times, so there was no reason for her to tap back twice.

Sara jumped awake at the sound of a heavy door slamming. She lifted her hand from where it hung off the side of the bed and grabbed for her phone on the nightstand. It was 8:00 AM.

When she heard Ian's familiar footsteps in the kitchen, she fell back onto her pillow and sighed. The dreams left her waking to a hollow feeling, and she dreaded another day of silence.

That was what had brought on the dreams. The silence of yesterday. The only time she'd ever been quiet around Ian was when he was comforting her.

That was another thing Ian didn't know about. He knew she hadn't been happy at home, but she'd never let on that her dad hit her. And her dad was always careful not to leave a mark. She'd known at that early age that Ian would've gone after her dad. Ian was protective of her to a fault, and he wouldn't have held back had he known.

She often wondered if the person who'd broken in

that night had been coming for her, and if her dad had meant to let her be taken.

Liz had snuck back into her house the next morning and dressed for school. When she walked into the kitchen, her dad was sitting at the table, but he'd looked at her as if he'd seen a ghost.

Now that she knew what all he'd really been doing at the Ritter Farm, she knew she was lucky not to have been taken.

The secrets were eating her up inside, and she wanted to tell her best friend. It was hard to start a conversation with him when it was clear he didn't even want to be around her.

Sara wiped the tear that snuck out from the corner of her eye toward her hairline. She closed her eyes and prayed.

Father, I need you to give me the words to say to Ian. I don't know when or how I should tell him, but please help me figure it out.

Ian

I an hadn't looked for Sara before making his way into the bathroom where he'd worked most of the day before.

There had been long hours of silence while they worked yesterday, and today was starting out to be the same. He hadn't heard a peep from Sara since he came in, and he hadn't made a quiet entrance.

The woman working just a few rooms away had been on his mind the entire day, and sometime during the mountains and valleys of his thoughts, he'd decided he should make a point to start calling her Sara. His Liz was gone, and calling her Sara made her a stranger.

She was a stranger, really. He didn't know Liz any more than he knew Sara, so what difference did it make what he called her?

He'd silently practiced asking Sara what she wanted him to pick up in town for dinner, or what she wanted for breakfast. In his mind, he'd asked her what she did for a living now and why she'd left in the night when they were eighteen years old.

He'd been installing the new flooring for half an hour before he heard the boards creak behind him where he crouched in the bathroom. He turned to look up at Liz—Sara—propped against the doorframe. Her hair was piled atop her head in a jumbled ball, and she wore an oversized T-shirt and sweatpants.

Ian was a little too dumbstruck to wish her a good morning. She looked innocent and guarded, and he could've sworn she was eighteen again.

"Sorry," she whispered. "I overslept. Can I have the bathroom for a minute?"

He stood, and she moved to let him pass.

Her soft voice drifted behind him. "You want me to make you some toast or a peanut butter sandwich for breakfast? There isn't much else I can offer you yet."

He turned to her, and she looked like she might burst into tears at any minute.

Ian's chest constricted. She looked tired, and he hated that this huge life change was probably hard for her. He didn't want her working on her hands and knees like she had yesterday, but the rational part of his mind said that she wanted this project to be finished so she could be rid of him. He hadn't heard a single complaint about the hard work.

Ian cleared his throat and looked away. "I'm fine. I brought you a breakfast plate from The Line. It's in the kitchen. I brought some things for the fridge too and stocked it."

He barely heard her whispered "Thanks" before her footsteps creaked into the bathroom.

A few minutes later, they'd passed in the hallway as he resumed his work. He was determined not to think about Sara today. A few times, Ian had been distracted when he'd heard her moving through the house, but he wouldn't lose sight of the reason he was here—to help Sara get that inheritance she wanted. Why she wanted it, he still didn't know.

Ian was cleaning up the newly installed flooring when Sara stepped quietly into the room in her socked feet.

"I made some sandwiches."

Ian checked his watch. It was after noon, and his stomach clenched at the mention of food. "I'll be right there. Just cleaning up."

Sara padded off toward the kitchen without another word, and he followed close behind her.

Two bottles of water sat on the small round table next to two paper plates. One plate had two sandwiches on it, while the other had only one.

Sara grabbed a bag of chips and set it in the middle of the table as she took her seat in front of the single sandwich.

Ian washed his hands and settled himself in front of the other plate. "Thanks for lunch."

"No problem."

The silence gnawed at him, and he wondered how long she'd make him wait. Would she ever tell him? He'd settle for anything. Any small glimpse into her life would've calmed the burning anxiety in his middle.

She didn't even look his way while she ate her lunch. Keeping her eyes on her plate, she bit, chewed, and swallowed in a monotonous circle.

They finished eating at the same time, and Sara grabbed his empty plate and threw it in the trash.

Ian stood to get back to work, but Sara stopped him with a demanding, "Sit."

He turned to heed her order as she picked up a book from the counter. He hadn't noticed it before.

She settled back into her seat and looked at him. Where had her happiness gone? He searched for it, but her eyes and lips didn't hold a single glimmer of joy.

When she just looked at him without speaking, he finally asked, "What are we doing?"

"We're having church," she said, finality lacing her words.

"Seriously? You don't need to have church just because it's Sunday," Ian scoffed.

He'd been the one to lead her to church and Christ

when they were kids, but now, he'd be the last tree to be known by its fruit. His had rotted a long time ago.

"I can't go to church now, but it's where I'd be if I had a choice," Sara said. "And the word tells us in the book of Matthew, 'For where two or three are gathered in my name, there am I among them,' so we're having church."

Ian huffed. "I don't think church is for me anymore."

Creases formed between Sara's brows. "You might be a sinner, but God is a forgiver. You're not so far gone that you can't come back."

He leaned forward and propped his arm on the table. "I know you say that, but it seems too good to be true. Sin and God don't mix, *Sara*." He made sure to emphasize her name. "I'm not sure He understands my troubles anymore."

She didn't understand. It *was* too late for him. He'd made his bed in a house of lies and lived there until it became his home. He'd turned his back on her and anything that was pure and good for so long. He couldn't ask to be forgiven after all the time that had passed.

Sara dipped her head and opened the Bible in front of her. "I'm pretty sure that's your fault. I've done a lot of things I'm not proud of, and He forgave me. When was the last time you talked to Him?"

Instead of waiting for his answer, she went on. "I've just been reading a chapter every day. If it's okay with you, I'll just pick up where I left off in Romans chapter fourteen."

Ian raised his hands in the air. "Don't mind me."

Sara tilted her head to the page before her. "As for the one who is weak in faith, welcome him, but do not quarrel over opinions."

Ian leaned back in his chair and closed his eyes. He'd given up on his faith a long time ago when the anger had taken control. How had Sara been able to hang onto it?

He wasn't focusing on Sara's words at first, but it was easier to listen than to tune her out.

Sara read on, "For none of us lives to himself, and none of us dies to himself. For if we live, we live to the Lord, and if we die, we die to the Lord."

Wasn't that what he'd always believed when he was younger? That you're never too broken to go home?

Too bad he was sitting next to his home, and everything good about it was broken between them.

When she finished the last word and looked up at him, he couldn't sit here with her any longer without knowing why she was doing this to him.

"Where have you been?" Ian asked.

Sara just looked at him, her chest rising and falling with each breath that filled the space between them.

Silence. Still no answers.

"Fine. You keep your secrets, and I'll keep my bad attitude. How's that?"

Sara's lips pursed, and her breathing quickened. He welcomed her anger. He deserved it. Her temper lit a fire inside him. He had so much to say to her, and all they'd done since she'd been back was dance around the things they weren't saying.

"What if you lose the attitude already?" she asked.

The *what if* game had been their way of communicating for as long as he could remember, and her use of their old tradition took the sting out of her harsh words.

"I don't have an attitude." It was a lie, and she would call him on it. He wanted her to. He wanted her to tell him he hadn't been worth her time and future then or now. He wanted her to put him out of his misery.

"Oh really? Grumpy is your default now? You're about as cuddly as a cactus. Where is my Ian?" she pleaded.

He couldn't stand this. He gripped the edge of the table. It wasn't right. They were always meant to have each other's backs. He *was* her Ian. At least he wanted to be.

"I'm just not a kid anymore," Ian said.

Sara scoffed. "Forgive me if I liked the boy better than the man. Is that your excuse for being my friend all those years ago? We were just kids?"

"No," he answered quickly. "I'm just not in the mood to be fooled twice."

Sara sat back in her chair and crossed her arms over her chest. "I did some things I'm not proud of, but how exactly did I fool you?"

She'd made him believe she loved him, but he'd just as well keep that thought to himself.

Ian grumbled, "It doesn't matter."

Sara threw her hands in the air. "What if I can't work with you like this?"

What if again. Ian shook his head. "Wouldn't be the first time you bailed on me."

"That's a cheap shot. You don't even know what happened!"

Ian sat forward, his irritation growing as he realized the power she had over him. "Exactly! Because you didn't tell me!" His nostrils flared as he tried to calm his racing heart. "We were kids, and we're not anymore. This is me now. Like it or not. If you can't work with me, I'll finish the house on my own. You'll get your money."

"I didn't say I wouldn't work with you. I said I can't work with you like *this*." She gestured between them. Her words softened as she reminded him, "We used to be friends."

"You pushed me away, Sara."

"I'm sorry. Is that what you want to hear?" She went on, and he sat frozen. "I should've chosen you. It was always you. I made a mistake that cost me twelve years of not seeing my best friend."

Tears rimmed her eyes, and the sight of her sadness

had his chest aching. She needed him, and he needed to go to her. He hated himself. It was a place he was familiar with now, but he'd never been so full of self-hate as he was in this moment.

Sara brushed a tear from her cheek and stood. "I don't know how to tell you. I'm scared to tell you, and I know it'll only make things worse. And when you're always mad and mean, I don't want to share anything with you. I don't owe you anything when you treat me this way. I want my Ian back, and so does God." She looked at him as if she pitied him. "It's lonely where you live with your anger day in and day out. When you decide to give it up and come back to me, let me know."

Sara stormed out of the room, and Ian couldn't form the words to grovel at her feet.

Come back to me.

He'd give anything to go back to her. Could he do that? Would she let him?

Ian called out after her, "Liz!" but her only response was the bedroom door forcefully closing, separating them again. He ran to the door and pressed his forehead against it.

"Liz, I mean, Sara." He might be messing that one up for a while yet. "I—"

"Not today, Ian. We'll talk tomorrow."

Her words held a finality that had him backing away from the door. Why was it so hard to just let her come to him in her own time? Maybe she would tell him what he needed to know if he wasn't pushing her away at every turn.

Whether it was his best friend or his Savior, he'd been sure for too long that he was too broken, and it was too late to be forgiven.

Brian had been right when he said that Ian wasn't what she needed. He didn't know how to give her the space to trust him again. Too many years and too much hurt lay between them.

Sara

S ara wouldn't let him see her cry, so she stormed off to her room like a coward. Ian had never upset her before, but there was a first time for everything now that she'd broken his trust.

She heard him call her name—her old name—and she almost turned to him before a fresh sob choked her and urged her on. She needed a barrier between them, so she closed the bedroom door with too much force.

Alone in the tomb she'd created for herself, she let the sobs break free. Once again, the decision she'd made to leave him behind hit her in the back like the sharp point of a knife. Why had she left him? In thinking that she was giving him the freedom he deserved, she'd bent a vital part of the man she loved—his faith. Any faith he had in her or the Lord was gone.

She understood why he was angry with her, but not God. There had been times in her lonely years that her relationship with Christ had been her only comfort. How had Ian abandoned his faith after all they'd been through together as kids?

The empty space in the room was too thick around her, and her anger—no, her fear—clawed at her insides. Tears of heartbreak sliced down her cheeks and left dark splotches on her T-shirt.

Desperate to feel something to dispel the void around her, she leaned her back against the door and sank to the floor. She'd hide out in here until he left this evening. She couldn't face him again today. The unspoken things between them hurt almost as much as his accusing barbs.

She never meant to hurt him.

There were plenty of things that needed to be done in this room. But she'd have to face him again tomorrow, and the next time she saw Ian Hart would be too soon. He hated her now, and it shattered her inside to see his friendship replaced with anger.

Grabbing the dresser for leverage, she lifted herself up from the floor. When she was standing, she noticed the note Mr. Garrison had left her. It lay an inch away from her hand, and she slowly reached for it. Would the words be the balm she needed right now, or would they deepen her sadness?

She touched the edge of the note and debated. She'd have to read it eventually.

Unfolding the note, she sat on the bed and read.

Lizzy,

I never told you about my life before you. I was almost sixty years old when you were born, and there was too much to tell.

I was a lot like you growing up. I didn't have bad parents, but my folks didn't have two cents to rub together. You were always a reminder of my childhood, and I've been praying for you since before your mom left. I always hoped you'd make it.

I made it out. I left when I was seventeen, and I got a job at a factory in Atlanta. Then I moved on to Birmingham. I went to college there and got a degree while I worked. I made my way across the southeast to Dallas and met a friend who would become my business partner. We started Garrison Corp., and business took off during the war.

After living the corporate life for decades, I was tired. I'd left a lot in Carson, and I was ready to come home. My parents were gone, and they'd left the house to me. It's the one I'm asking you and Ian to work on. I didn't go back there often, but I allowed a few friends to stay there over time, and they kept it up.

Dover Lane seemed as good a place as any to retire and live a quiet life by myself. That was what I thought I wanted until you, Ian, and his brother came along. I resented you for disrupting my solitude for a while. Then, I was fascinated. I watched you playing together, growing, coming to love each other, and you brought me back to life. I started to care for you, and that made all the difference.

I was slipping into my death before you came along. After you, I was alive again. You and Ian kept me going.

I wanted things to be different for you, Lizzy. I wanted you out of that house, but I wanted you to choose Ian. You didn't know it, but that boy loved you. Devotion like that is rare, and I never wanted you to go through life alone like I did.

I don't want you to regret the life you lived. I'm proud

of how you faced the hard times life threw at you. I don't know anyone who could've done it like you did. I just wanted you to know that you had more than me to lean on.

You saved me, and I can't thank you enough for that. I have more money than I know what to do with, and I can't think of anyone I'd rather give it to. I know you want to help people who can't help themselves, and I want to do what I can to help you.

Just one thing. Be patient with Ian. Give him time to heal, and then be patient some more. He isn't the same boy as he was when you were young.

Yours,
Nathaniel Garrison

Her tears smeared the words on the page, and she blotted them with the blanket on the bed beside her. She always knew there was more to Mr. Garrison than he'd told them, and she wished the letter was longer. She needed more of her friend.

Tilting her head up, she studied the room. This was the house Mr. Garrison had grown up in. Had this been his bedroom or his parents'? The place was so isolated. Living on Dover Lane must have reminded him of the quiet woods.

She and Ian had certainly not been quiet. They'd played in Mr. Garrison's yard more often than their own lawns. It was the middle ground, and their shared neighbor hadn't run them off.

Be patient. She could be patient, but her heart was tired of running. She needed to tell Ian what happened so they could move past it or let it destroy what was left between them.

When her emotions had run dry, she set about working in the bedroom she'd locked herself in. She cleaned out drawers, hung blinds and curtains, and dusted everything from the ceiling to the baseboards.

Ian left without a word when darkness fell, and Sara breathed an easy breath. Her stomach rumbled, and she ventured into the kitchen for dinner. Settling on a simple turkey sandwich, she gathered the bread, mayonnaise, meat, and cheese before looking around for a paper plate. Ian must have moved them today while he was measuring the countertops to replace them.

After a brief scan of the open counter space, she spotted them near the microwave beside a bag of chips and a bag of candy. She shoved the candy bag aside, but then she paused.

Butterscotch—those hard candies Mr. Garrison loved. He'd always had a glass bowl of butterscotch candies on his kitchen counter, and Sara had loved them too.

The tears burst from her anew. Ian hated butterscotch, but he'd bought them for her anyway.

She gripped the bag and let her renewed grief flow from her in waves that shook her body. She grieved for Mr. Garrison. She said good-bye to her friendship with Ian. And she mourned the life she could've had if she hadn't become a witness to a federal crime.

It was too much in one day. She wanted a redo—of the day and the last twelve years—but she knew by now that she had to live with her consequences. There were so many things in her life she wished she could change. The night she'd changed her friendship with Ian, the night she'd officially ruined any chance they had of being happy together, the night she'd left him behind.

All of those choices were tied together, and they'd led her here—to this lonely house in the woods where she just wanted to crawl through Ian's window like she had when she was a kid and let him take all of her pain away.

Ian had previously protected her from things like this, but since her decision to leave, she had learned to be strong and face the fears he could no longer help her carry.

Why was it so much harder to be strong when she was close to him? Why did it seem impossible to protect her heart from the beating it took each time he rejected her?

Sara wiped her tears and sucked in a long breath. Tears were worthless. She could never cry enough to put out the flames in her life.

Shoving the bag of candy to the side, she grabbed a paper plate and turned to make her dinner. She knew she'd be all right. That was what she'd learned from all of this—that she could overcome the terrible things in life on her own.

She would be all right, just not tonight.

Ian

I an sat in his truck outside of Rusty's and read the letter again. It'd taken him over forty-eight hours to open Mr. Garrison's last words, and Ian wished he'd waited longer. He wanted to crumple it up and throw the old coot's sentiments out the window. Instead, he'd read it a dozen times since.

He missed his friend. Mr. Garrison had been a constant in Ian's life, and he wasn't ready to let the old man go. They had lunch together every week, and he wasn't sure what he'd do with his Tuesday afternoons now.

But he did know. He'd be spending every hour of daylight at Sara's place until further notice. His productivity floundered when she was close-by. He made rookie mistakes and had to redo more measurements than he had since learning fractions in grade school.

He tossed the letter into the passenger seat and looked out the windshield at Rusty's. The local bar and restaurant was family friendly until nine, and his friends liked to hang out here. Brian, Leah, Addie, and Lindsey were on the regular entertainment rotation, and they always called him to join them when someone had big news to share.

Ian was tired of hearing his friends get all excited over engagements and babies. Tonight, it was Jake and

Natalie, and he would bet his last month's pay that they were expecting their first kid.

He could leave—refuse to go in. He liked to think they wouldn't notice if he didn't show up, but he knew Natalie would cry and Jake would show up at the hardware store tomorrow with his hands on his hips.

Ian shut off the truck and slammed the door with a little too much force as he got out. Best to just make an appearance and get it over with. He could sneak out while the happy couple were busy being congratulated, and no one would notice.

He moved through the night like smoke in a fog. He knew how to keep his head down. He just rarely put the skill into practice. It was easy to let his negative opinions fly at his friends.

Sure enough, after the plates were cleared, Jake stood from his seat, and their side of the restaurant got quiet except for the kids. His crowd took up most of the main room now, since families had started to grow. Ian was the only one without a herd to call his own.

Jake turned to Natalie, and she stood and wiggled in close to him. Jake's booming voice filled the room. "We have some news."

Sissy stood and yelled, "Congratulations!" before Jake or Natalie elaborated.

Natalie burst into tears, and she was immediately swarmed by the women around her.

The news about babies was always the worst. Sara never knew how he felt about her before she left, but he'd always imagined their future together. It was inconceivable to picture a life without her.

Ian had always assumed she cared about him, but they hadn't ever said the words out loud. "I love you" had always been a silent truth between them. And he did love her. He loved her more than a man full of anger should ever be able to conjure.

They hadn't even talked about dating, but neither of them had dated other people... until she left.

Ian hung his head in his hands. This could've been their life. Engagements and weddings and babies. They would've had a happy life together. He was certain of it.

And after watching Liz Jennings—now Sara Williams—grow up with him, he knew he wanted kids with her. He wanted to grow old with her.

But then she'd left, and his future faded into blackness.

He stood fast and his chair scraped against the wooden floor as he swerved around the chairs and tables toward the door.

A heavy hand grabbed his arm, and he reluctantly turned to see who had a death wish.

It was Jake, eyes bright and ready for battle. "Don't leave."

Jake's eyes narrowed, and Ian knew exactly what his friend was feeling. He'd spent too many years protecting the woman he loved to not recognize the man in the mirror. It would hurt Natalie's feelings if Ian left now, and Jake would try to stop him.

"I can't stay here," Ian told him, willing his friend to leave it alone.

"You're never gonna get past it if you don't accept that you can't change what happened."

Ian jerked his arm away from his friend's grasp. "I got this." He tilted his chin toward the hustle and bustle at the table. "Get back to your party."

Ian turned for the door without looking back. Jake didn't understand. None of his friends did. Happy moments like this weren't made for Ian. He wouldn't ever have things like this to celebrate and people who loved him hanging around slapping him on the back in congratulations. Not one of his friends knew what it was like to know you messed up and there wasn't hope of a redo.

He'd gone over that last day he saw Sara in his head a million times. She'd been happy with him. She'd sat on the porch swing with her head leaned on his shoulder. His arm had rested on the back of the swing behind her.

"What if a bunny runs out in front of your car and your dad swerves to miss it, and he loses control and hits a tree?"

Ian laughed. "You're really morbid." They played the *what if* game a lot, and Liz was never one for practicalities.

"I'm just scared you won't come back." Her whisper was carried by the wind as they pushed the swing in tandem.

"What if I come back and everything is the same as it's always been—me and you against the world?" He leaned his head back and took a deep breath, letting the smell of fresh-cut grass tingle in his nose.

Of course, his Liz wouldn't be pacified. "What if you get dragged out to sea by a rip current?"

Ian let his thumb brush over the back of her hand where he held it in his lap—the only place they really touched. Anything else was crossing into dangerous territory—a place they hadn't been before that would push their friendship. "What if I stub my toe on the table leg and I need emergency surg—"

Liz slapped him in the chest. "Stop making fun of me, Ian. You know I don't know what to do without you."

"Yes, you do. Just steal some candy from Mr. Garrison. Everything is better with candy."

Liz slapped him again. "You're the worst."

"I think you're mistaken."

Liz lifted her head and turned to him. Their lips were inches apart, and he noticed that her gaze went straight to his mouth.

He'd tell her when he got back. He'd tell her he loved her and wanted to spend the rest of his life with her. He didn't want to do it now. All her talk of ways he could die had a bad taste lingering in his mouth. He couldn't leave her with that.

He knew exactly why she was nervous to see him go. "I'll leave the window cracked. Don't chance it while I'm gone. Just go ahead and plan to stay at my place."

She stared at him and bit her lip. He hated leaving her more than she hated seeing him go.

"I promise, the next time I leave, you'll be going with me." He'd been working summers and evenings for years with Joe Masterson doing odds-and-ends jobs to save every penny he could for after graduation. They'd go wherever she wanted. She wouldn't be scared anymore. They'd find jobs and apartments and hopefully still live close to each other. Maybe one day, she'd agree to marry him.

If Ian made it until graduation without knocking the living daylights out of her dad, he'd take Liz away from here and she'd never have to worry about anything ever again.

He didn't have any proof that her dad hit her, and he'd asked her countless times. But if he ever got word that her dad had laid a finger on her, Ian might not wait for the proper authorities to handle the job.

Ian slid into his truck and slammed the door. That was twelve years ago. Everything had been right. How could she have left without him?

She ran away from you. She didn't love you.

Ian huffed in the quiet cab and shook his head. Of course she didn't love him. Sara was everything good in this world. Sweet smiles and a heart of gold. Sugar and spice and everything nice.

He gritted his teeth as he started the truck. He was hard lines and jagged edges. He'd only ever been good at one thing—protecting the love of his life. But when it had all boiled down, she'd left him and never looked back.

Ian sped out of the gravel lot, slinging rocks in his wake. No, none of his friends knew that kind of rejection. He was the one who had to live his life knowing he wasn't good enough.

If she wasn't going to give him answers, maybe he needed to be the one who laid it all on the line. He could tell her how devoted he'd been to her, and maybe she could understand why it had ripped him apart when she'd left.

He wasn't sure where he was going until he was leaving Carson's town limits. The one person who meant more to him than any other was less than a ten-minute drive away, and he couldn't turn his truck in any direction that didn't take him closer to her.

He'd left today without saying good-bye. He hadn't apologized, and he needed to make things right. He needed to make everything right, but he wasn't sure if that was possible anymore. She said they could talk tomorrow, but patience wasn't his strong suit, and he didn't want her going to bed another night without knowing he was sorry.

He wanted to kick himself for not being gentler with her. Ian had never been harsh with her like that before, and he didn't want to do it ever again.

He wasn't sure why he was acting like he didn't have anything to lose. He had everything to lose now that Sara was back.

His heart wasn't made of stone when it came to her.

Sara

Sara spread out the curtains Ian had bought for the bedroom windows. They weren't bad at all. She might have picked them herself, if she'd been able to shop. She rubbed the thin material between her fingers. The design was light gray with darker gray flowers and white accents embroidered in vertical rows.

Maybe she wouldn't have chosen these, after all. They looked and felt expensive. She would've certainly taken the price tag into consideration while shopping.

Sara didn't have expensive tastes. She wondered if Ian did or if he'd just thought she would like them. She *did* like them. The room was dark with its wood-paneled walls, but the gray was light enough to brighten the small space. They were also thin enough to let the sun shine through. She liked to wake at sunrise on days when she didn't have to be at work.

She missed her job. She'd been working for Memphis Mission before she'd gotten the phone call from Andrew. That call had changed the trajectory of the life she was living.

Andrew had told her about Mr. Garrison's death, and he'd been patient while the shock of her grief imploded. They'd talked about what Mr. Garrison's death meant for her. That's when he'd asked her to come back to Carson for an indefinite amount of time.

The next day, she'd been weighed down with grief when she told her boss and co-workers she needed to leave. The lack of notice was hard on the team, but they'd been supportive as she prepared to pack up and meet the next chapter of her life.

Sara strung the rod through the curtains. Working on the house with Ian was rewarding in its own way, but she missed helping the families. Interacting with people and giving them hope and motivation was something she loved.

She needed to ask Andrew about the plans for Mr. Garrison's house once they were finished with the renovations. If she would be allowed to use it for the shelter, then this place could change lives once it was finished. Most women seeking refuge with the shelters where she'd worked came with nothing but the clothes on their backs and children if they had them. A place like this could be groundbreaking for a family just getting started.

Leaving the curtains on the bed, she stretched her arms above her head to see if she would need a chair. She could touch the rod hanger, but she wouldn't be able to get the rod over the hook and adjust them.

She picked up a chair from the kitchen and heaved it under her arm as she carried it to the bedroom. After positioning it to the side of the window, she turned to grab the curtains.

A crash outside the window had Sara turning on her heels to face the intrusion. A rustling ensued, and Sara backed away from the window into the nearby corner.

She might as well have been sitting in a fishbowl. The room was tiny enough that, if whoever was out there peeked in, she'd be seen. Why hadn't she put the curtains up sooner?

Her pulse beat wildly in her ears as she scanned the room for her phone. Where had she left it?

She spotted it on the dresser and spared one look toward the window before scurrying on her hands and knees across the room, the uneven boards grating against the bones in her knees.

Grabbing the phone, she crawled to the other side of the bed and crouched down. The banging outside started again as she pressed Ian's name on her phone.

He answered quickly. "Hey."

An informal greeting to begin a phone call, but she'd take it. "Ian, I think someone is outside. I hear lots of noises." The gun she'd brought with her from Memphis was still in the glove compartment of her car. A lot of good it would do her there. She'd always kept a weapon close, but Ian had been here earlier. He seemed as good a weapon as any, and she'd forgotten to arm herself when he left. "I don't have a weapon."

Ian's tone was stern, but it didn't hold the usual sting. "I'm on my way. I'll be there in two minutes or less. Stay hidden and stay on the phone with me."

"How can you possibly be here in two minutes?" she whispered.

"I was already on my way," Ian said.

Sara furrowed her brows. "How did you know something was up?" She lifted her head above the bed and looked out the window. It was useless. There weren't any lights out there, and it was fully dark.

"I didn't. I was just on my way over."

Sara was at a loss for words. She wanted to repeat her question, but it was clear he wasn't going to answer it. "Thanks for coming," she whispered.

Ian's deep voice sent a warm rush down her spine. "I'll always come when you call."

She hadn't been certain he'd come at all, but her insecurities and doubts had been overridden by her need for a helping hand. Knowing he was willing to come running at a moment's notice eased her aching heart.

"I'm coming up the driveway. I don't see anything in the woods, but I'll check around the house."

"Okay, do I need to stay on the phone?" she asked.

"Yeah. You don't have to talk."

"Okay," Sara whispered. "We'll just listen to the sounds of each other's respirations." She heard his truck door shutting through the phone and outside the house.

Ian's chuckle was quiet, and he whispered, "You're an odd bird."

"I won't deny that."

His playful tone reminded her of the fun they used to have as kids. She'd always spoken her thoughts, and Ian hadn't minded. Instead, his voice had been filled with awe as he reminded her that she was unique without wounding her self-esteem. He seemed to like it that she was a little different.

She heard leaves crunching outside of the window, then a rustle and banging.

"Ian!" She all but screamed into the phone as she stood and ran for the door. In that moment, she didn't care that she was defenseless. Ian was out there, and he needed help.

Holding the phone to her ear, she unlocked the back door with shaky hands and threw it open. She took one step onto the porch and saw Ian standing just past the railing.

"What's going on?" she asked, as if he should've begun his explanation sooner.

Ian pointed toward the forest. "Raccoons. They found an opening beneath the porch and two of them were fighting." He crouched to inspect the hole. "I'll patch this up tomorrow after I can make sure there isn't anything in there that needs to come out."

"Raccoons." What a goof. She'd called him and made a huge deal out of a couple of coons.

"Yeah, I don't know if they'll be back tonight, but I think you're safe."

Thankfully, he wasn't giving her a hard time about making a big deal out of nothing. She wrapped her arms around her middle to shield against the cold. "You wanna come in?"

Ian

Ian followed Sara into the house. She moved into the kitchen, and he followed her. She wore no makeup, and her hair hung loose over one shoulder.

Everything he wanted to say to her had built up inside of him. He wanted to tell her he was sorry and that he loved her. He wanted to wrap her in his arms and kiss her like he should have done years ago.

He tapped his knuckles on the table three times. Their code would have to change from touch to sound until she trusted him again.

Sara gifted him a closed-lip smile and tapped her knuckles once on the counter.

When he couldn't hold it in any longer, he breathed, "I never wanted to let you go."

Sara nodded and bit her bottom lip. "Me either."

All the things he'd been dying to hear from her were meaningless. Those two words were enough for him.

Ian fought to control his voice as he said, "Everything that happened between us—and everything that didn't happen—feels like forever ago, but then, it feels like yesterday."

In truth, nothing felt real anymore. Seeing Sara again had been only a dream for so long, it was hard to reconcile the reality that she was here. The painful separation from her that he'd endured felt like his eternal punishment for not being enough for her.

Sara cupped his face in her soft hands. Tears brimmed in her eyes as she confessed, "It wasn't so long ago that I've forgotten you. You were never far away from me. What happened to you?" she whispered.

Ian shrugged. "It killed me—losing you. I thought we would always have each other, and then suddenly, you were gone, and I just knew it was because I'd messed up."

"No, Ian, you never messed up. I'm so sorry you felt that way."

"I couldn't think of another reason for why you wouldn't talk to me anymore. I called and texted you constantly."

"I had to give up my phone. I never got those messages."

She had to give up her phone? Why?

He needed to be patient. Hopefully, he'd find out soon if she could understand why he'd been so angry and hurt. "Nothing mattered after you left. I don't feel anything anymore."

That was a lie. He felt everything too deeply, and that was his curse. He needed her too much, and it had hurt too deep when she left.

Sara's eyes narrowed as if she didn't believe him. "I'll just keep being nice to you until you feel it."

His heart beat too forcefully against the wall of his chest. "Feel what?"

She threw herself at him, wrapping her arms around his broad shoulders.

He braced himself, and then let her body melt into his. Sliding his arms around her, he could breathe again —full, healing breaths that gave him the courage to lift her off her feet and closer to him.

One arm wrapped around her body while his other

hand wound into her hair and cradled her head. He didn't resist the urge to lean his cheek against her dark waves. All the anger and fear that had wrapped its roots around his heart fell away.

"I don't want to fight," Ian whispered in her ear. "I hate it when you cry."

Their relationship had always been innocent before. Ian had controlled his desires for years when it came to Sara because she'd meant too much to him to risk losing her.

Now, he burned for her, and she melted in his arms. Everything was different, but everything was the same. No matter what they had gone through to get to this moment, he still loved her unconditionally.

"I'm so sorry. I messed up so bad, and I don't know if you'll forgive me. I missed you so much," Sara cried into his shoulder.

He held her tighter still. "I missed you too."

Ian had wanted to hold her like this for so long. As much as he had wanted her to crawl through his window every night when he was sixteen years old, he recalled the lack of sleep he'd gotten in his youth. That's when he felt his protective love growing into more, and it had taken everything he had not to tell her he loved her.

He hadn't minded sleeping on the floor back then. It was being so close to her that had kept him up at night. She would hang her arm off the bed, and he was intensely aware of how beautiful she was. Things were changing, and it had terrified him. Her hair spread out on the pillow, and he could smell her citrus shampoo. Even on those nights when she didn't come over, there was always a reminder.

For months, he'd stared at the dark ceiling of his bedroom from the safety of the floor. How could he keep things the same between them? How could he keep her in his life for always?

She'd touched him too much. Just innocent touches, like bumping into each other, and he was sure she didn't know how it affected him when she brushed her fingertips over his arm or rested her hand on his shoulder while asking for his opinion. He had aced every class in high school after resorting to studying every night she slept over. Only physics and calculus could distract him from wanting more with his best friend.

Ian had been captivated by her in high school. He had no chance of resisting her now that she was a woman.

Sara pulled away from him and brushed the tears from her face. "I was so scared back then. I didn't know what I was doing, and I thought I was doing the right thing."

Ian pulled her back into his chest. "Stop. Not tonight." Something had shifted between them, and he wanted her to stop crying before she told him anything. "We can talk about it in the morning. You're tired, and I just came to tell you I'm sorry. I was a jerk today—and every other day. I'm sorry. If you still want to tell me tomorrow, we'll take the day off and just talk about it."

She nodded against his chest. "I'd like that." She leaned back in his arms and wiped her tears on her shoulder. "Would you mind picking up a small rug for the living room?"

Ian pressed his lips against her forehead before releasing her and stepping back toward the door. He held onto her hand for a moment longer. "Of course."

Sara wanted something from him, and old habits die hard. Denying her anything she wanted would never make its way onto his to-do list.

She tilted her head to the side and asked, "What do you think we're supposed to do with the house when it's finished?"

Ian was stupid enough to hope that she'd stay here. Only until he could tell her how he felt and pray for the first time in years that she felt the same way. If she did, he'd marry her tomorrow, and he didn't care what they did with this house.

"I'm not sure. Maybe Andrew knows." He tilted his chin to her as he grabbed the doorknob. "I'll see you in the morning. Get some rest."

Her shoulders relaxed, and she let her delicate fingers slip from his grip. "See you in the morning."

Ian walked through the dark night back to his truck. The light from his phone lit up the cab. Three missed calls and two texts. All from his sister-in-law. He decided to check the messages first, since they would probably tell why Sissy had been trying to reach him.

Sissy: Where are you?

Sissy: Call me.

His sister-in-law was never short and sweet, and a wave of fear washed over him. He hit her number on his recent calls list.

Sissy answered, "Hello."

Skipping the greetings, Ian asked, "Is everything okay?"

"That's what I wanted to ask you."

Ian had almost forgotten about leaving Rusty's in a mood after Jake and Natalie's announcement. "Yeah, I'm fine. I just—"

"I get it," Sissy cut him off. "We just worry about you."

"Thanks, but there's no need. I already have a mom."

Sissy had been mothering Ian and his friends for years before she married his brother and had kids of her own. "Good."

It was strange to hear Sissy short of words. He'd prepared himself for bad news or a tongue lashing.

"I'm fine, Sis."

He *could* talk to someone, but Sissy wasn't his first choice. Plus, he had sworn to keep it a secret that Sara was back in town. Even if she didn't go by the same name, Sissy had known Liz back then from school, and Ian had only been hung up over one woman in his life.

Sissy sighed, "Tyler is worried. It wouldn't hurt to call him or stop by for dinner one night."

He wanted to spend his dinners with Sara, but it might be a good idea to dispel any suspicions by making an appearance. "Yeah, I can stop by tomorrow afternoon."

Sissy perked up. "Good, I'll make your favorite."

"What's my favorite?"

"Anything with meat." Sissy's tone had lost its worried edge.

Ian laughed and disconnected the call. With only a few more miles to home, he called Jake.

His friend answered after only one ring. "This is a call I wasn't expecting."

Ian almost flinched, until he realized he deserved the jab. "I'm sorry I didn't stay tonight. I know it meant a lot to you and Natalie."

Silence followed Ian's apology.

"Jake?"

"Sorry, I'm just... Thanks. It means a lot that you called."

"Is Natalie around?"

"She's right here."

"Can you put her on the phone?" Ian asked.

A scratching sound filled Ian's ear as Jake passed the phone to his wife.

Natalie answered, "Hello?"

He couldn't blame Natalie for the hesitation in her voice. Ian's apologies had been few and far between for a long time now.

"Hey, it's Ian. I just wanted to tell you I'm sorry I bailed at dinner tonight. Congratulations."

Natalie began whimpering, and Ian kept quiet.

"I'm sorry," Natalie said through her tears. "I'm just so happy."

Ian was happy for them, but he couldn't erase that twinge of jealousy that still sat in his gut. "I know. You and Jake are gonna be great parents."

"Thanks, Ian," Natalie whispered.

"Can I shout at Jake again?"

"Sure. And I'm sorry it's tough for you. I get it." Natalie sniffled. "I really hope you find someone who makes you happy."

"Who says I'm not happy?" Ian asked.

Natalie laughed. "Here's Jake."

"Hey, man. Thanks for that," Jake said in greeting.

Ian rubbed a hand over the stubbled hair on his head. "No problem." It really wasn't as hard to be nice as he made it out to be.

"To what do I owe the change of heart?"

Ian huffed. Of course, there must be some outside force interfering if he was being nice to his friends. Come to think of it, why were they even friends with him when he was grumpy most of the time?

When Ian didn't answer, Jake guessed. "Is it her?" he whispered. "How's she doin'?"

"As good as can be expected, I guess," Ian said. "She's puttin' up with my pleasant disposition."

Jake laughed. "Be good to her. I feel like I don't need to tell you that, but—"

"I know, I know. This is my second chance. You don't have to tell me."

"Right. You got this." Jake's words were anything but sure.

"I'm trying. I really am."

"I can see that." Jake paused. "You were different with her. I'm not saying she makes you better, but you do seem happier with her."

Jake was right. Ian's black heart felt less toxic when

he was with Sara. She was the light in the darkness. "I am."

"Listen, if I'd known where she was or what I could do to bring her back—"

"I get it. I was a little heated when she came back to town, and I took it out on you. I'm sorry."

Jake chuckled. "Save it. I'm not your friend because it's easy, but someone's gotta do it."

"Tough job." Ian thought about how much tougher it would be for Sara to love him, but the selfish part of him hoped she was up to the challenge.

Sara

The next morning, Ian brought more than just a rug for the living room. He brought a few decorations and more groceries too. All of her favorite foods were pulled from grocery bags one by one, including more butterscotch candies.

"You didn't have to do all this," Sara said.

Ian glanced at her with a smirk. "Yes, I did."

She pulled the contents from the next bag. "You brought pancakes too?" The tray was from The Line, her favorite diner in town. He'd been stopping by there a lot this week.

"Of course."

"You know I can cook, right?"

Ian chuckled. "I know you're a good cook. I just don't want you to cook if you don't have to."

She felt a rush of warmth in her chest. This was the Ian she'd known, and her heart didn't ache so badly now that he wasn't throwing darts at her. He knew that she'd spent her childhood taking care of a dad who hadn't appreciated her. Cooking had always been a chore to her—something else that had to be done.

They sat down across from each other at the small, wooden table and began eating without ceremony. "So, what do you do now?" she asked around a mouthful of pancakes and syrup.

"I own the hardware store in town." Ian looked up from his plate. "With Brian. You remember him?"

"Of course, I remember. You *own* the hardware store? That sounds huge."

Ian shrugged. "It's a big business, but Brian and I balance everything out. He's the pretty face, and I'm the brains."

Sara laughed, and her mood lightened. "That sounds about right."

"He's been taking on a lot more while I'm out, but he doesn't mind." He gestured to her with his fork. "What about you?"

"I'm in between jobs right now." She lifted her brows to him as if it were obvious. "But I guess that doesn't matter if I can't go out to spend any money. I'm a youth counselor."

"No kiddin'?"

"No kidding," she confirmed. "When I left Carson, I spent quite a lot of time in therapy." She turned her attention back to her food. Why not confess to your love interest that you've been seeing a therapist? She had to remember that Ian was her friend, not her boyfriend. "I got my degree in behavioral science from the University of Kansas."

"So, you've been in Kansas all this time?" Ian asked.

"Nope. I was only in Kansas for two years. Before that, it was Ohio, and I finished high school in Texas."

Ian had cleaned his plate in record time and set his fork on the empty Styrofoam container. "Wow. You did a lot."

"I moved a lot in the beginning. Then I settled down in Memphis and got a job. I've been there since I graduated from college." She moved the pieces of pancake she'd cut up around her plate with her fork. "I guess I grew a lot when it seemed like nothing was happening. Those years were slow."

She lifted her head to him and smiled. "Looks like you grew a lot too." There wasn't much denying he'd grown. He was built like an oak tree, thick and tall.

Ian sat back in his chair and studied her with a smirk.

She smiled and licked the syrup from her lips. "Why don't you tell me about what you've been up to while I finish eating?"

Ian shrugged. "Not much to tell. I joined the marines, got married, got divorced, opened the hardware store, and here I am."

Sara coughed and tried to dislodge the hunk of pancake she'd inhaled when he said he'd been married. "Back up a little. You got married?"

"You remember Julie York?"

Sara's eyes widened. "Yeah. From Carson High School? You married Julie York?"

"Well, in case you forgot, you were my prom date before you up and left me." Ian rolled his eyes. "Julie found out you were gone, and she jumped at the chance —the next week."

Sara dipped her chin and stuffed another bite into her mouth.

"So, I agreed. I was mad, and she wouldn't let it go. I gave in and went with her. She was a little pushy, so I let her boss me around for a while and demand dates. I didn't really care about anything."

Sara didn't interrupt. Maybe if she just kept quiet and chewed slowly, he'd keep talking.

"After a few months, I thought I'd made it clear I was joining the marines after graduation, but that didn't deter her. She just dug her claws in and said she'd wait." Ian lifted one shoulder indifferently. "The first time I came home, she was there, and she wanted to get married. So, we did."

Sara was wrapped up in the story. "That's it?" It didn't sound like a very romantic relationship, but she kept that thought to herself.

"That's... basically it. She wanted the wedding, and it was easier to just say yes. Every day felt like borrowed time when I was with the marines, and I didn't care much about anything. Life was just happening, and I was just... existing."

His words broke her heart. Her Ian had been so full of life, and it killed her that he had spent that time trudging through life. Not only that, the unwelcome jealousy of his marriage to Julie was clouding her judgment.

Sara wanted to ask what had ended his marriage, but she didn't want to be too forward.

Ian stared at her for five, then six heartbeats before he said, "I was medically discharged when I broke my foot. I wasn't in a good place. The marines were the only thing I had left." Ian took a breath and said, "I came home, and she was pregnant."

Another wave of pain shot through Sara's middle. She didn't want to hear any more. The pancake and syrup mixture threatened to rebel in her stomach.

"I hadn't been home in eight months. She was six weeks pregnant."

"I'm sorry," Sara fumbled to find more comforting words. "That must have been horrible."

Ian shrugged. "She wanted a divorce. She'd met someone else and wanted to be with him."

Sara set her fork down and stood. Ian watched her as she walked around the table toward him and gently shoved his shoulder.

He pushed his chair away from the table and stood, allowing her to wrap her arms around his middle.

"It's okay. I wasn't a good husband. I tried to be angry at her, but I wasn't really. I was mad at myself, and

I wasn't over losing you. I just gave her the divorce she wanted and went about my life."

Sara swallowed the hurt in her throat. "I'm sorry, Ian. I always thought you would be a great husband. What happened?"

There was silence before he whispered, "I lost you."

Sobs broke from her, quick and angry. "I'm sorry. I'm so sorry for everything."

Ian held her tighter. "No, I'm sorry. I'm sorry I wasn't what you needed... or what you wanted. I'm sorry you had to do it alone."

"No, Ian." Sara wiped her eyes. "I need to tell you everything."

Ian cradled her face in his hands and looked into her eyes. "I really don't want you to be crying when you tell me. I understand now that you haven't talked about it because it's hard for you."

He wiped the tears from her cheeks with his thumbs, and the callouses scratched against her sensitive skin. "What if I made us some coffee and we sat on the back deck? I tested it last night, and it's sturdy enough to hold us until I can get around to rebuilding it."

Sara couldn't help but relax at the words *what if*. "That sounds good. I'll help you make the coffee."

"Why don't you find us some blankets? It was chilly when I got here an hour ago."

Sara smiled and nodded. "Okay, teamwork."

Sara

S ara didn't have to look far for the blankets. There was one on the couch and one on the bed that she'd been throwing over her feet at night.

She stepped out the back door onto the porch to find that Ian was right. The wind was blowing, and the early spring breeze slashed at her cheeks like knives. She wrapped the blankets around her shoulders and surveyed the backyard. The trees were still leafless, and only faint patches of sky shone through the forest canopy.

The rebirth of spring hadn't taken hold here yet, but it would come in the next few weeks. Until then, she could brave the cold winds for this view. Surrounded by trees and far away from anyone she needed to hide from, the woods held a comfort she craved. Had Mr. Garrison played out here as a kid?

Sara turned to examine the deck, and while it seemed sturdy enough, there wasn't anywhere to sit. She stepped back inside and grabbed an old chair from the living area. It was wooden with scrolling arms and padding on the seat and back with a red and turquoise paisley pattern. Had the mismatched furniture belonged to Mr. Garrison's family? How old could this chair be if Mr. Garrison was almost ninety years old when he died?

She set the chair on the porch and threw the blankets on top of it. Intent on grabbing another chair, she almost bumped into Ian as he stepped onto the porch.

"Whoa. I saw you grabbing chairs." He was carrying a chair from the kitchen table under one arm and the handles of two mugs of coffee in the other hand.

"Here, let me help with that." Sara carefully took the cups from him while he positioned the chair beside the other.

Ian grabbed the blankets and gestured for her to sit down. She balanced the cups as she sat, and he draped a blanket over her legs before sitting in the other chair and adjusting his blanket.

He had moved his chair toward hers until they were touching, and she passed one cup of coffee to him.

"Thanks," Ian said as he accepted the cup. "I didn't ask how you like your coffee."

"Black is fine."

Ian huffed and the corner of his mouth turned up in a grin.

"What's so funny?" she asked.

"Of course you like it black. You've never made a fuss over anything in your life, have you?"

Sara feigned offense. "What does that mean?"

"It means you don't like putting people out. I bet you've never asked a barista at a café to put anything extra in your coffee before because you'd hate to inconvenience someone."

Sara rolled her eyes. "It's not just that. I just don't need anything extra."

"Have you ever *wanted* anything extra?" Ian asked.

The truth wasn't as simple as "Yes, I wanted to try creamer once." The honest answer was that wanting simple things led to wanting bigger things, and there were big things she didn't want to hope for only to have her dreams crushed.

She had wanted more than friendship with Ian in high school. She had wanted him to kiss her and hold her like the other girls had done with their boyfriends. She had wanted a life with him.

But those were big things that were out of her reach. Ian had been a normal kid, and as much as she wanted to think she was normal, there wasn't anything normal about her family life and what her dad had done.

She ignored his question and blew the steam from the surface of her coffee.

"What do you want to do with that money?" Ian asked.

Another question, and thankfully, she didn't mind answering this one. "I've worked at a few non-profits that help women and children."

Ian nodded. "Well, that makes sense."

Sara inhaled the scent of her coffee before taking a tentative sip of the hot drink. "Yeah. There are a lot of them, fortunately, but none around here. When I was going through all that, I had you. Most people don't have anyone, and that terrifies me."

Ian had turned his body to face her now, giving her his full attention. "Did he hit you? Tell me the truth."

He'd asked her the same question countless times. Sara sucked in a breath, and the cold air bit at her lungs. She knew Ian was asking about her dad. "Yeah."

When Ian didn't say anything, she turned to him. His eyes were blazing, and a shot of fear ran down her spine. He would be mad at her for lying to him all those years.

Ian was leaning on the arm of his chair, and his hazel eyes were a foot away from her—intense and beautiful. "I told you I'd take care of him."

Sara tilted her head as if addressing a child who didn't understand the unfairness of the world. "I didn't tell you because I know what *take care of him* means. I wasn't willing to lose you."

"You shouldn't have stayed there!" Ian sat back in

his chair, filled with anger. "We could have found a way to get you out."

"And that would've meant moving in with a foster family who knows where." Sara flung her hand into the air. "It wasn't that bad, and it would've been worse if you hadn't been two doors down."

"Anything would've been better than living with him. He didn't deserve you." Ian pounded his fist on the arm of the chair. "I don't care where you would've gone. I would've found a way to be with you."

Ian's confession was a balm to her wounded heart. He'd always been intensely loyal to her, and she'd broken his trust when she left him. She reached for his hand, and he released the fist he'd made. When he was relaxed, she linked her fingers with his.

Ian tapped his finger three times on the back of her hand. His silent question, letting her know it was okay to stay quiet. *Are you okay?*

She tapped back once. She was okay. Come what may, he deserved the truth.

Sara gathered her nerves to tell him everything that might finally sever whatever bond they had left. "Before I tell you, I just want you to know that I'm sorry."

Sara

L iz finished scrubbing the pot she'd made the chili in earlier. She'd have plenty to freeze since Dad didn't come home for supper and Ian was on vacation with his family. It didn't look like anything was missing from the surplus she'd made.

The old house was quiet, save for a few creaks here and there. Her phone dinged with a text, and she pulled it out of the pocket of her sweatpants as she passed the back door. Her dad's filthy boots caught her eye, and she tucked the phone back into her pocket. It was Ian. No one else texted her. Right now, she needed to get those boots cleaned off and outside.

She scrunched up her nose at the smell of chicken manure and grabbed the top of the boots as she opened the door. She kept a wire bristle brush by the back door, and she sat on the cinderblock step and held her breath against the stench to brush the bottoms.

Mr. Garrison's back porch light was on. He always left it on... for her. The old busybody knew she snuck over to Ian's sometimes, and she'd been sleeping over there while he and his family were on vacation.

She slept much better at Ian's house. She didn't have to worry about anything there. Most nights, she knew Ian was close-by, ready to stand between her and any danger. Even when he was gone, the walls of his house felt like more of a fortress than hers.

Her phone rang, and she stretched her leg out to the last step so she could dig the phone from her pocket. It was her dad.

"Hello."

"Lizzy, I need you to come pick me up at the Ritter Farm. Buck was supposed to be my ride, but he left early." Her dad's southern twang really kicked in when he mumbled his curses at Buck.

It was nearly 10:00 PM, and she really wasn't looking to drive to Bradford and back tonight. She sucked in a deep breath and regretted it. The chicken poop smell lingered.

Everyone knew what went on at the Ritter Farm. She'd just scrubbed the evidence off the bottom of her dad's shoes. The McCalls fought roosters, and her dad was always right there in the middle of it.

Liz hated it, but she wasn't the one calling the shots around the house, even if she was the one who carried a lot of the responsibility.

"Be there in thirty," Liz said.

Her dad hung up the call without any thanks. She hadn't expected it. Expectation wasn't the root of *all* heartache, but there was a possibility of at least some indigestion if she ever got her hopes up.

Liz changed from her sweatpants into jeans and threw on her old New Balances. She remembered Ian's text as she slipped into the driver's seat of her dad's pickup. Liz and her dad only had one vehicle, but she did most of the driving because her dad's license had been expired since she turned sixteen.

Ian: It's raining. Mom is making us play Old Maid.
Ian: Send help.
Ian: SOS
Ian: What if I die of boredom? That's a real thing. I'm sure of it now.

Liz chuckled and texted him back.

Liz: What if you hang in there for a couple more days and come home to me?

She started the truck while she waited for his answer. Adding those last few words had been a bold move, but he'd been pushing the limits of their friendship lately, and she wanted to play too.

Ian: I can definitely manage that. I miss you.

Liz smiled into the darkness and shifted the truck into gear. Thirty minutes later, she was pulling up at the Ritter Farm. She parked close to the McCall house, even though she knew her dad would be in the barn out back. She needed to pee, and she hoped someone in the house would let her use the bathroom.

Liz ran through the dark night to the house and knocked on the door. After dancing on the balls of her feet for a minute, she knocked again. "Hello!"

She was doing the pee-pee dance like a toddler now, and she performed the pleasantry of knocking once more before she tried the knob. It wasn't locked, so she stuck her head inside.

"Hello?"

The house was quiet. She knew Kenny McCall lived here, but she didn't know of anyone else who might live with him.

She took a tentative step into the house and scanned the room. The brown walls and brown carpet made the place look like a mirror image of her own house.

Tiptoeing toward the hallway, she guessed right the first time for the bathroom. First door on the right.

Minutes later, she felt relieved and snuck back out into the hallway. As soon as she emerged, bared for all to see, a rustle in one of the rooms had her searching for a way out. Grabbing the doorknob beside her, she turned it, but it didn't open. She shoved her shoulder into the door thinking it was jammed, and it gave way suddenly, as if it had been locked and the latch had slipped.

Liz fell into the dark room and realized too late that the rustling had come from inside.

"I'm sorry. I'm so sorry," she stammered. "I was just looking for a bathroom."

The rustling intensified, and Liz stopped scrambling backward to listen.

It was humming. A frantic hum, not a sweet, peaceful hum.

Liz scrambled for the light switch and flipped it. She squinted to let her eyes adjust to the sudden brightness.

A young girl who looked to be about Liz's age lay on the floor. Her ankles were tied together with rope, and her wrists were secured behind her back. Dark-brown hair fell over most of her face, but Liz could make out the rag tied around the girl's mouth.

When the girl lifted her head, Liz could see her red eyes and tear-stained face.

"What in the world?" Liz rushed to her and pulled the rag from her mouth. "What are you doing here?"

"I don't know! These two men came into my house and took me." The girl gasped for air and wiggled where she sat on her hip. "You're the first person I've seen besides them."

Liz stepped around the girl and fumbled with the knots on her wrists. "How long have you been here?"

"Just a few hours, I think. They haven't been back since they put me in here. Please hurry."

Liz's fingers slipped over the rope. If she could just stop the trembling, she might be able to get them both out of here before Kenny McCall came back.

"I'm working on it. What did the men look like?"

"One of them might have been in his forties. Dark hair. Kinda fat around the middle. The other one was younger and skinny." Her words shook with her body.

That sounded like Kenny and Owen McCall. Liz fished for her phone in her jeans and dialed 911 before sticking the phone between her ear and shoulder. She picked at the knot for half a second before a woman said, "What's your emergency?"

"Hey, I'm at the Ritter Farm off Cherokee Creek Road, and there's a girl here who says she was kidnapped. I'm untying her now, but her wrists are bleeding, and she's scared."

"Do you have an address?"

"No, but there's a big white sign at the turnoff that says 'Ritter Farm.'"

"Does she need medical attention?"

Liz looked at the girl and noticed the blood on her head. "I don't know. I just found her. She was locked in a dark room and tied up. She's got some blood on her head."

"I'll send an ambulance too. What's your name?"

"Liz Jennings."

"I'm connecting to Bradford Police Department now. Can you hold?"

"Sure." The knot on the girl's wrist finally gave slack. "What's your name?" Liz asked her.

"Trisha."

The woman on the phone caught her attention again. "Ma'am, the Bradford Police are on their way. Can you stay with her until they arrive?"

"Yes, I'll stay." Liz's hands were shaking as she pulled the rope from Trisha's wrists. Liz disconnected the call and started working to untie the knot on Trisha's ankles.

Trisha raised a shaking hand to the spot of dried blood on her head. "He hit me before he tied me." Her voice shook with her sobs. "I think I was out for a minute."

"It's okay. The police are coming." This was the last straw for Liz. She'd kept her mouth shut about the Ritter Farm for too long to protect her dad, but she'd never turn a blind eye to this.

The thud of heavy boots and the slamming of a

wooden door had both girls paralyzed. Listening, and not daring to breathe, they waited.

"She should be here already."

Liz recognized her dad's voice, and she wished she'd thought to close the door to the bedroom. They were sitting ducks.

"Grab a beer. I'll be back."

Kenny McCall's voice drifted down the hallway, and Liz was spurred back into action. She fumbled frantically at the knot. They had to hide, but there wasn't enough time. He would walk by that door any second and see them.

"Stay quiet," Liz whispered to Trisha. As if that would help them.

In the panicked waiting moments, Liz prayed to the sound of her heart beating.

Lord, please send help quick. He'll kill us both.

Liz knew Kenny would. He fought roosters he had shipped in from overseas. Her dad often went with Kenny to pick them up.

A wave of nausea hit Liz's stomach just as Kenny's broad frame filled the doorway.

He meant to put Trisha on one of those boats. Kenny was selling people, and Liz was sure of it. Just as she was sure that she and Trisha were cornered. They would either be killed or Liz would be on that boat right beside Trisha.

"What are you doin' in here?" Kenny took two lumbering steps into the room before backhanding Liz so hard she fell into the corner.

"Dan! Get in here! I found your stupid daughter."

Pain slashed across Liz's cheek, and Kenny was making his way for Trisha as Liz's dad barreled into the small room.

"Stop!" Liz threw herself at Kenny and latched onto his arm, leaning her whole weight on the limb to prevent him from getting to Trisha.

"Lizzy! Get outta here!" Her dad's fury burned in his words when he saw her.

"Get a handle on your daughter, Dan!" Kenny seethed as he flung Liz to the floor.

"Dad! Stop him!" Liz yelled.

When she turned to her dad, his mouth was set in a scowl, and his brows were furrowed. He turned his attention from Trisha to Liz.

"Dad!" She knew her pleas were lifeless. Her dad would only see her as a liability now. She'd seen too much and gotten in too deep to leave here alive.

Ian

Ian's insides churned as Sara continued her story. It took everything he had not to vomit in the bushes beyond the deck railing.

Sara went on. "The cops came, and I remember hearing them at the door and screaming until my lungs hurt. They got my dad and Kenny, but Owen wasn't there, and even with my testimony about what Trisha had told me, he wasn't convicted. There wasn't anything to tie him to what happened, except Trisha's word."

Standing, Ian leaned against the deck railing to face her. He'd been quiet throughout the story, but every emotion warred inside him. Anger, rage, disgust, fear. What had happened to her was worse than he'd imagined.

She was beauty from ashes, a flower rising from a crumbled ruin. She was resilience in human form, and it was a miracle that her small shoulders could bear the weight of the pain of her past.

"The cops finally took me home after I gave statements, but I asked them to take me to Mr. Garrison's house. I couldn't go home alone."

Ian let his chin fall to his chest. He'd always been

there for her when she didn't feel safe at home, but this time, he'd failed her. He'd failed when it mattered most.

"Sheriff Tubbs was there with me when I told Mr. Garrison what happened. They decided that they weren't going to wait for the federal government to step up and offer me protection. Turns out, Mr. Garrison had friends who could pull strings and get whatever he wanted. I agreed to testify as a witness, but Sheriff Tubbs warned me that the case against Owen McCall was threadbare. He'd never be convicted, and I'd always be the one who put his uncle away and tanked the cock-fighting gig. My dad and Kenny got twenty years to life for a handful of felonies."

She'd be facing the end of her twenty years sooner than she knew. The inevitable terror waited in her future. What kind of a life had she lived knowing it was all just borrowed time?

Ian rubbed his hand over his head and his chest rose and fell with his deep breaths.

"Mr. Garrison and Sheriff Tubbs worked together to find a place for me to go that night. It was almost morning by the time I left."

"And I wasn't there for you," Ian added.

"No, listen." She set her coffee mug on the deck beside her chair and pushed the blanket from her lap into Ian's chair. Standing, she took the few steps that separated them. "I could've told you. You could have come with me. I told them not to tell you." Her words faded into a whisper at the end of the confession.

"Why?" It was all his throat would allow to escape. The one question he wasn't sure he wanted to be answered.

Sara wrapped her arms around her middle against the wind. Ian wanted to go to her. He wanted to keep her warm and make her feel safe, but he was confused. Did she want his comfort or not? She'd left him behind intentionally.

Ian cleared his throat when she didn't answer right away. "Why didn't you let me come with you? I thought the plan was to leave Carson together. I'd have done anything to be with you. I'd have worked every hour to provide for us and make sure you were safe."

"That's the thing." Sara stepped toward him and lifted her chin to look up at him. "You would've done all that for me, but I couldn't kill you to save myself." She lifted her hand and let her soft fingertips brush against his cheek. "You would have done stupid things to protect me. I didn't want to hold you back. If I left and you stayed in Carson, I thought you would join the marines like you always wanted."

"The marines didn't mean as much to me as you did." The men in his family had been marines for the last three generations, and Ian had wanted to continue that legacy, but it was true that the job didn't hold a candle to her.

"You would've dropped everything to go with me. You had a shot at the future you'd always wanted. I couldn't take that from you."

Ian shook his head. Why couldn't she understand?

Sara continued. "And at some point, I needed to learn how to protect myself. I was eighteen, and it was time I learned how to handle my own problems. I had spent my life running to you when things were tough, and I needed to know that I was capable of looking out for myself. I wanted to know that I could do life without relying on you every single day."

Ian set his jaw and laid his heart on the line. "I never wanted to know a life without you. I didn't want to spend a *day* without you, much less twelve years."

Sara smiled. "You were always saving me. I couldn't do anything without you. I didn't *want* to do anything without you. I knew that if I didn't go that I would live my life under your wing of protection, and I'd never fly on my own."

Ian shifted his weight to his other foot. "Why didn't you tell me you felt like that? I always knew you could do anything, but I didn't want you to have to." Ian reached down and grabbed her hand in his. "I didn't want anyone or anything making your life harder than it already was. I could've backed off."

Sara shook her head, and he ached to touch her silky brown hair. "No, that's not in your nature. You're a protector, and despite what I just said, I love that about you. It just meant that I would never be a protector. I wanted to be stronger for myself before I would ever feel worthy to grow and do things like have kids that I would have to protect and nurture one day."

"That's not true," Ian said. "You took care of your dad even when you were little. I never doubted that you'd be an excellent mother. I knew you would do anything for someone else, even if that person didn't deserve it."

Sara shrugged one shoulder and her mouth tilted up on one side. "I needed to learn, and I did. And the dynamic between my dad and myself was... different. It was a love born out of obligation. He needed me, and I took care of him because I was tied to him and he had no one else. Sound familiar?"

"No," Ian admitted as he stroked his thumb over the palm of her hand.

"I didn't want you to feel obligated to love and care for me because you felt sorry for me." Sara tugged her hand away from him and pressed her fingertips to her lips. "I knew that kind of love with my dad, and it would kill me if you felt that way about me."

Ian wrapped his arms around her and pulled her close. "No, that wouldn't have happened to us. I know you didn't need me, but I wanted you."

He stroked her hair and tried to relax now that she was in his arms. How could he possibly make her understand?

Ian sighed. "Even back then, I knew what we had was different. When I found out you were gone, I was confused. About where I was going in life. About us. I can't remember if we were starting or ending when you left. All I knew was that I lost a part of myself when you left, and it changed me."

"I'm sorry. I made a mistake. I did grow and learn a lot while I was away, but I missed this. I missed you. And I can't get that back. How could you ever forgive me?"

"Shh," Ian whispered. "I do forgive you. I already have. It's over. We're here together now." The nagging question he'd been avoiding reared its ugly head. How long would they be here together?

"Why are you back here? How is it safe enough?" Ian asked.

Sara leaned back so she could look up at him. "Mr. Garrison told me Owen moved to Arkansas years ago. I stayed well away from Georgia while he was here, but he was the only rogue we knew about. Kenny and my dad are still locked up."

"So, with a new name and twelve years behind you, you're hoping that Owen isn't actively pursuing you?"

"Right. He's never made a move for me before, and I was able to live a normal life as Sara Williams. I just thought it was wise to lay low here, in case there was anyone in town who would recognize me and get word to Owen somehow."

Ian tried to let her words encourage him, but they only solidified his fears. "I don't trust him."

Sara laughed and wiped her face. "Of course you don't. I expected nothing less."

"It kills me every time I think about him getting close to you. I can't see anything except red."

"You've known for all of fifteen minutes. It sounds like troubled times."

Ian hugged her tighter against him. "You have no idea."

"I wish things could be normal between us," Sara whispered.

Ian leaned closer to her, testing the waters between them. He wanted to kiss her, but that was a step they hadn't taken before now, and he didn't know what things would be like between them after that.

Could things be normal?

Two decades of repressed desire churned beneath his skin, and he was leaning in closer. He would stop if she pushed him away, but he couldn't stop on his own now.

"Sara." The whisper of her new name danced on his lips as he tilted his head slightly.

"Yes."

He barely heard the word, but he'd seen her lips move, and that was enough. His mouth crashed against hers, and his hands gripped her waist as he forgot to breathe. There was wind, and fire, and his heart was beating too hard against his chest. Her lips slid over his, and her chest was flush against him. He'd been missing this for so long, and the urgency in him was slow to settle.

He kissed her with the intensity he'd been bottling up for over a decade, and he didn't want it to end.

His need for her didn't end, but Sara pulled back from him after a few minutes. He lunged for her mouth again, claiming it again in a short kiss that stoked the flames inside of him in the same way the longer kiss had.

She giggled and pulled away again. "I can't breathe." She laid her hand on her chest. "It's just..." Her smile was bright as she said, "I've just wanted this for so long."

Her eyes glistened with unshed tears, and he pulled her into his arms again. "Me too. I've wanted to be with you for as long as I can remember."

After a pause, Sara said, "I think I need something

to drink." She lifted her head up and brushed the pad of her index finger over his lips.

His world was on fire.

Sara's smile was conspiratorial. "Before we do that again."

Ian

The silence of the last few days had been eradicated. Sara told him about high school while he installed the new countertops in the kitchen, and he told her about their old friends over lunch. They moved the furniture in the living room, and she started painting the walls while he finished up in the kitchen. The rooms were close enough that he could read her facial expressions when he looked her way.

Ian's phone rang at 4:30. It was Sissy, and she barely let him answer the call before she started in on him.

"We're having lasagna. Be here at 5:30, and please don't be late because I had no idea how hard it would be to make lasagna with a toddler and an infant." A crash in the background was followed by a childish scream.

"I'll be there." He'd forgotten, but he refrained from thanking his sister-in-law for the reminder that he'd promised to stop by for dinner.

"Good. Bring some rolls. I'll throw them in the oven when you get here."

"Yes, ma'am."

Ian caught Sara averting her gaze as he disconnected the call. "That was Sissy. I promised her I'd stop by for dinner tonight."

"Sissy? Dakota's sister?"

"Yeah, she's married to Tyler."

Sara's eyes widened. "Really? Your brother? That's surprising."

"I know. At the time, it came as a shock to everyone." Ian leaned back against the fridge and crossed his arms. "Now, I can't imagine one of them without the other."

"We didn't talk much about your family."

"I know. We have plenty of time though. I'll tell you about everyone tomorrow." And the next day. And the next day. He wanted to be doing this with her for an endless number of days.

Sara smiled and went back to brushing the paint onto the wall. "That sounds good."

Ian made his way into the living room, and she placed the paint roller into the tray and stood to meet him.

Ian rested his hands on her hips and released a deep breath. "I have to go. Sissy wants me to stop by the store, and I need to check on Brian at the hardware store."

Sara wrapped her arms around his neck. "I know. We can't hide out here forever."

He wanted to. They were making up for lost time, and he wanted her to keep talking to him. There were too many years he'd spent without hearing her voice.

"I'll be back in the morning. I'll text you when I'm on my way, and you can let me know what you want for breakfast."

He leaned in and let his lips seal with hers. The last thing he wanted to do was leave.

Pulling back, he said, "I think I'll just call Sissy back and—"

"No, sir. You're going to dinner, and you're going to have fun, and I'm going to see you in the morning." She let her arms slide from around his neck and down the collar of his T-shirt. "I'll be here."

"I'll call you tonight," Ian promised.

"Okay, just go. Don't be late."

Ian jumped into his truck. A gnawing feeling to stay tugged at his middle. Now that he knew what had happened all those years ago, he didn't feel comfortable leaving Sara here alone. He had always been her place to run if she felt scared, and leaving her didn't feel right.

At the least, he was installing a security system on the old house tomorrow. At best, Sara might agree to let him hang around later or even stay over. There was an extra room, after all.

He pulled up at Tyler and Sissy's house at 5:25 and handed the pack of rolls to Sissy when she met him at the door.

"Thank you. I'm starving, and dinner is ready. Tyler and the kids are in the garage. Can you call them in?"

"Sure." Ian turned on his heels before entering the house.

He stepped into the garage and Lydia spotted him first. Jace was still too young to notice.

"Uncle Ian!" Lydia jumped up from the floor where she'd been playing with a doll and ran for him.

"There's my girl." Ian wrapped her in his arms and twirled her around.

Lydia framed Ian's face with her tiny hands. "Mommy made lasagna."

"I know. I'm here to tell you it's ready to be eaten."

Lydia's face showed exaggerated surprise. "Let's go!"

Ian carried her inside while Tyler followed carrying baby Jace.

Within minutes, Lydia was leading the blessing, and the whole family was digging into the lasagna. Ian listened as the family told stories about their day and the things that had happened. Sissy had taken the kids to the park, and Lydia made a friend. Tyler told them about having to upgrade the registration system at the office.

Sissy turned to Ian and asked, "So, what's up with

you? I stopped by the hardware store today and Brian said you weren't there."

Ian finished chewing his bite and nodded. He never took time off work. Before Sara rolled into town, work kept him busy enough to distract his mind.

It was strange, but Ian thought he'd been more settled than usual in these days he'd been away from work. It wasn't like him to take his hands off things at the office and delegate, but Brian and Lindsey hadn't called him once.

Sissy wouldn't be put off by a non-answer. "I've been working on a project with a friend lately."

Ian was bursting to tell them about Sara. He finally had something good in his life he valued enough to share with his family and friends, but he couldn't. For once, he wished he could talk to Sissy. She always knew what to do when it came to people. Ian wasn't under any delusions that he was a perfect man, but was he good enough to even ask Sara to give him a chance?

The lasagna turned sour in his stomach. How long would they have to keep Sara's presence here a secret? What if she couldn't ever come out of hiding? If she needed to move because Carson was too close to whoever might be looking for her, he'd move with her. Brian would buy him out of the hardware store, and he'd follow her wherever she needed to go. He couldn't lose her again.

"A friend?" Sissy asked. "What friend?"

"I have friends," Ian countered.

"Not friends that I don't know about," Sissy pointed out.

Tyler reached across the table and took his wife's hand. "Ease up on him. He doesn't have to tell us."

Ian knew Sissy didn't like secrets, and he wondered how far she'd take her push when her eyes narrowed at him.

"Fine," Sissy quipped. "I'd love to know more about this project, if you feel like telling me."

He didn't, but he knew he'd have to throw her a bone. "It's a home renovation. I won't be at the hardware store as much." Come to think of it, Ian wasn't sure how long he'd be out of work. Granted, Brian was managing fine without him so far, but it'd only been a few days.

Tyler jumped in and started telling Ian about their local fishing club's upcoming tournament, but his thoughts were in the woods with a woman who had the wheels in his head spinning.

Sara

The next morning, Sara woke before the sun. After a dreamless night, she jumped from the bed well-rested and ready for the day.

After showering and adding a little makeup, she started a pot of coffee. She was moving furniture around in the living room to get started on her painting for the day when her phone rang. It was Trisha.

"Hey, stranger," Sara said with a smile as she placed the phone between her ear and shoulder.

"I know. Sorry it's been so long. Were you up?" Trisha sounded tired but happy.

"I was." Sara looked around at the house Mr. Garrison had grown up in—the house she was living in until further notice. "I don't even know how to begin to tell you where I am."

Trisha sighed. "I need to unwind, so start at the beginning."

Trisha had taken the stand and testified against Kenny, Owen, and Sara's dad after her kidnapping, but Trisha hadn't let it break her. She'd moved to France with her mother a few months after the sentencing, and she'd entered the criminal justice field. Trisha lived a physical life that involved long hours in the gym along with the regular training required for her job.

Sara laughed. "Well, I'm back home."

"You're where?" Trisha asked, all exhaustion gone from her voice.

"Yeah. You remember Mr. Garrison? He died last week, and now you're talking to the heir to a billion dollars."

"A wha—" Trisha gasped.

"Well, probably half of that after taxes and whatnot."

"Sara! You didn't tell me that old man was a bajillionaire!"

Sara laughed. "I didn't know! I knew he always had plenty of money to give me for college and whatever I needed until I got a job, but it seems that old coot was keeping some secrets."

Sara trusted Trisha with everything. They'd weathered too much together not to have each other's backs.

They'd both endured countless hours of therapy after their unfortunate meeting, and they'd quickly come to be a sounding board for each other. No one else could quite understand what they'd been through together.

"I can't believe this. You're back in Carson?"

"I know. I never thought I'd see it again."

Trisha asked, "Is it the same?"

"Would you believe me if I told you this place is stuck in time? Downtown hasn't changed a bit."

"I'm so glad I moved. There was a learning curve, but I feel like I was always meant to be here."

"You were," Sara agreed. "You must be French at heart."

Trisha scoffed. "Tell that to the people around here. I hardly have an accent anymore, but I'll always be an American."

Sara laughed. "That Southern twang is hard to get rid of."

"Tell me about it."

There was a beat of silence before Sara sprang on the topic she really wanted to talk about. "Ian is here."

Trisha gasped. "What? Tell me more." She knew all about Sara's past with Ian. Trisha had comforted Sara through her tear-filled nights after she left Georgia and Ian.

"Mr. Garrison left us a house to fix up. Once it's ready, I can have the money, and I can finally open the shelter here."

"Oh, friend," Trisha gushed. "I can't believe it's happening. That's what you've always wanted."

"I can't believe it might actually happen. Things with Ian were tough at first, but I think we're moving past the hurt."

There was static on the line as Trisha moved around. "What did he say? Was he mad?"

"Oh, he was mad. Livid better describes his attitude when he found out I was back and that Mr. Garrison knew where I was the whole time."

"Your life is so interesting," Trisha whispered dreamily.

"You know it's bad to wish for an interesting life." They both preferred the quiet life after the bout of turmoil that had shattered their youths.

"I know." Trisha yawned. "But sometimes it beats work, eat, sleep, repeat."

"You have the best life," Sara reminded her. "Don't get it twisted."

"I do. Paul is good to me. I never thought I would trust someone like I trust you and Mom."

Trisha married Paul a few years back. Her job transferred her to a new district, and she quickly fell head over heels for her new neighbor.

Sara whispered, "I'm so glad you're happy."

"Yeah, remember when I thought moving to France was the worst?" Trisha asked.

Sara shook the gallon can of paint and chuckled. "Remember when I said I'd never go back to Carson?"

Trisha whispered, "Life never turns out like we want."

"But God has a plan," Sara finished.

Sara was prying the lid off of the paint can when a knock on the door startled her, sending her heart racing.

Ian's deep voice was muffled through the door. "Sara, it's me."

"I have to go. He's here."

"It's not even 7:00 AM where you are," Trisha pointed out.

"I know. He usually doesn't get here until closer to 8:00."

"He's got it bad."

Sara laughed. "Gotta go."

"Call me back when he leaves. I'll be up."

He was early, but she wouldn't complain. She was eager to see him after their breakthrough the day before. Her heart was still pounding against the wall of her chest when she unlocked the door and opened it for him.

The smile on Ian's face was bright and infectious. He didn't spare a second for greetings as he moved into the kitchen and threw the bags on the counter without breaking their gaze.

She moved back to let him into the room, but he was keeping step with her. His hands framed her face, and his mouth met hers in a sweet greeting. She breathed in his clean smell and relaxed against him. He was warmth and comfort and home.

Being near him reminded her of who she was. She was still the same Liz he'd known before, but she'd changed in some good and bad ways. He was reminding her with a loving kiss that her heart still belonged to him, and his belonged to her.

When they broke the kiss, Ian released a contented

sigh. "I missed you. Not just since yesterday. I've been missing you like crazy for years. I love you. Loving you was easy. Missing you was the hardest thing I ever did. I don't deserve you, but I'm selfish, and I—"

Sara's heart swelled. She'd been waiting years to hear those words.

She leaned back and stuck her finger over his lips. "Stop right there. I don't know what makes you think things like that, but love is patient and kind."

"I know the love chapter," Ian said.

"Then you know that love protects."

Ian eyed her but didn't respond.

Sara went on. "Love believes, hopes, and endures. Sound familiar? I've never heard that love is selfish, and I don't think I ever will. It's not selfish of you to want to be loved." She smiled and rubbed a hand down his cheek. "If you know me at all, you should know that I always loved you."

Ian wrapped her in his arms, crushing her to his chest. "I meant to tell you twelve years ago."

He breathed deep, allowing her to hear the steady beat of his heart where she rested her head against his chest in the silence.

"I think that's why I was so mad at myself," Ian said. "I didn't tell you sooner. And nothing ever changed it. My love didn't leave when you were gone. It just... stayed and reminded me of what I'd lost."

"Oh, Ian." Her heart broke as he crushed the air from her lungs with his embrace.

"I know I'm hard to love, but if you'll give me a chance, I'll love you right this time."

Sara chuckled. "You did it right the first time. I don't recall love ever being *wrong*."

Ian leaned away from her and gave her a ghost of a smile that hung with shame. "You're all I ever wanted." He brushed her hair behind her ears and studied her face as if committing it to memory. "I don't know where you have to go after this or what the future holds for us, but I want it to be us together. If you have to leave because it's safer somewhere else, I'll go with you. I just want you in my life."

Stunned, Sara nodded. "Okay," she whispered. Of course he would go with her. He should have gone with her the first time. She'd taken so much from him.

"I missed you," she breathed through her silent tears. "And missing you meant missing a part of myself. We were always meant to be together." She placed her hand over his heart. "We're bonded. We did that early on in life. Those ties don't break easily."

"I can't believe you still want me," he whispered. "After the way I've acted."

"I told you, no one is too far gone to be forgiven," Sara reminded him.

"I know. I really do. I've just been telling myself I'm a lost cause for so long, I started to believe it."

Sara pulled back to look up at him. "You scared me the other day. You're the one who took me to church and made sure I learned about Christ. My faith has held me up in some of the worst times, and it breaks my heart to think that—"

Ian interrupted her, "I won't lie to you and say that I've been a model Christian since you left. I haven't. I've been an example of what not to do, but..." Ian rubbed a hand over his head and huffed. "I know you're right. I should be in church. I shouldn't have given up on God. I couldn't ask you to share a life with me knowing that I didn't intend to be the man of God that you deserve."

A weight lifted from Sara's chest. With the burden gone, her heart soared.

Ian cupped her face in his hands. "I'll be a better man. You deserve better, and I want to give you every-thing. I always did. Can you forgive me?"

"What if I already did?"

Ian grinned. The sweet grin that he only shared with

her where the left corner of his mouth tilted up. "I'll never deserve a woman like you."

Sara swatted his chest. "What did I say about talk like that?" She turned to the kitchen. "I made coffee."

"Good. I brought pancakes."

"I'm so lucky." Sara smiled and grabbed for the bag containing the trays of pancakes from The Line.

"You can't go outside, but you have a grumpy beast ready to do your bidding. So lucky." Ian rolled his eyes and followed her into the kitchen.

Ian

They ate breakfast slowly, savoring the ease of each other's company. How long had it been since he'd stopped and enjoyed anything he was doing? Now, everything he did with Sara by his side was exciting.

"What's on the agenda today, boss?" Ian asked.

Sara brushed her long brown hair behind her shoulder and pointed toward the living room. "I thought I'd put the second coat on the living room walls. What about you?"

"I think I can finish up the kitchen cabinets today, and then I plan to install a security system."

Sara's eyebrows rose. "You think we need that?"

Ian leaned his elbows on the table. "I think I'm not taking any chances when it comes to you. I didn't know the risks before. Now that I do, I'd sleep better at night if you had a security system."

Sara shrugged and picked up her plate as she stood. "Suit yourself. I won't look a gift horse in the mouth. Plus, a security system feels like an extension of your never-ending protection." She gifted him that smile that brought him to his knees.

His chest tightened as he blurted, "And I think I should start staying here if that's okay with you."

Sara dumped her Styrofoam plate in the trash and turned to him. "What?"

Ian stood and went to her. "I just want to be close. There's another bedroom I can sleep in. I'll give you your space." Only an arm's length lay between them now, but he was afraid to go to her. To keep his arms from reaching out to her, he scrubbed his hands over his head. It was slick after he'd shaved it this morning.

"I—" Sara looked everywhere except at him. "Are you sure?"

She hadn't said no, and that was more than he'd hoped for.

"I'm sure I want to be wherever you are. I'm sure I want you to say I can stay." He averted his gaze to the floor. "Just don't ask me to sleep on the floor beside you. I can't be *that* close."

Sara laughed and pushed his shoulder. "You can stay. I like that. It'll *almost* be like old times."

"Yep. I still won't be getting any sleep."

Sara shoved the cup of coffee she'd just poured at him and winked.

Ian watched as Sara walked off into the living room with her coffee, leaving him to get started on his kitchen project. She'd said yes, and he could breathe again.

After lunch, Sara dumped their plates into the trash and brushed her paint-stained hands on the sides of her jeans. "Let's go outside for a while. The paint smell is making me lightheaded."

Ian scooted his chair from the table and followed her. "Sure."

Sara headed for the back door and bent down to slip her tennis shoes on. "I haven't seen much of the property. Didn't Andrew say there are twenty acres?"

"I think that's what he said. I wasn't paying much attention to him that day," Ian admitted.

Sara stood and Ian followed her out the back door. The midday sun was bright, but the air was still crisp. He wished he'd grabbed his cap out of his truck before they started on this adventure.

They stepped off the back porch together, and Sara turned back to him. "I hear water. It sounds like there's a river close-by."

"That way." Ian pointed east.

"How do you know?" Sara questioned as she bounced with each step down the slight incline.

He grabbed her hand. "The lay of the land. The terrain slopes this way."

They fell into a silent walk with only the crunching of sticks and leaves beneath their feet rustling in the woods.

Sara spoke first. "Tell me more about what happened. I know everything about you up until eighteen, and then I know so little. Tell me more."

Ian's voice was like gravel scraping over concrete. "You don't want to know who I am without you. Trust me."

"I do trust you, but I also know you can't scare me off. Just spill it."

The sound of the rushing water grew louder as they entered a clearing at the bottom of the hill. The grass was greener with clovers and spots of white dandelion tufts near the bank.

Sara crouched down to pluck a dandelion then blew the seeds into the air. "I told Mr. Garrison once that I wished things were as simple as making a wish on a dandelion. You know what he said?"

Ian turned to her but didn't respond.

"He said I should pray instead. Dandelions die. Prayers are constant."

"Wise man," Ian said.

Sara turned to him, and her smile lit up her face like the sun. "So, tell me a story. Anything."

For years after Sara left, Ian had focused on what he'd lost instead of where he should be going. He knew early that he wanted a life and a family with Liz. He needed to show her that all men weren't terrible husbands and fathers. He spent his youth thinking about how he could be the best for her and any kids they might have.

Then, she'd left, and he'd tried to form a shadow of that life with someone else. Julie had been his lesson. She'd taken a fragile dream and shattered it. Or maybe he hadn't put enough into his marriage. He'd made a vow to someone, and neither of them had treated it with the care it deserved.

His ex-wife had known he wanted a big family. Ian loved his brother, Tyler, and they'd been best friends growing up. Ian's circle of important people was small, but it was powerful. He had Liz, Mr. Garrison, his brother, his parents, and a handful of friends he could count on. When Liz left, he'd stormed off with the marines. Fulfilling his family legacy was more to keep his mind off the things he didn't want to dwell on at that point.

He didn't want to talk about Julie or the marines. Maybe he should start with Mr. Garrison. She'd be interested in him.

"When I settled back in at home, I dropped in on Mr. Garrison. I hadn't been friendly to him in years." Ian snuck a side glance at Sara to gauge her reaction. "I thought he knew where you were, and he just wasn't telling me."

Sara shrugged and gave him a tight-lipped smile. "Guilty."

"I was awful to him, and he didn't tell me to hit the road when I kept coming back to hound him about you."

Sara crouched to pick up a jagged rock on the bank. "I didn't know you asked about me. He never told me."

"You thought I wouldn't ask?" Ian scoffed. "I lost my temper with the old man before I left to join the marines, and then I picked right back up where I left off after Julie decided she wanted out."

Sara winced.

"Sorry," Ian whispered. "I was a hothead. To be honest, I still am. I've been angry for a long time, and it's hard to forget that feeling."

Sara stood and let the rock tumble from her open palm into the river. "I'm sorry."

Ian waved her off. "I think we're past that now. And I'm pretty sure I'm the one who owes a million apologies."

Sara shook her head.

Ian continued. "Mr. Garrison finally sat me down one day and told me I had to focus my anger into something constructive. He'd watched me spiral in my sorrows long enough."

Sara tilted her head, intrigued.

"He told me to think about a business venture I'd be interested in. I should direct my attention to something that could better my future. He agreed to fund whatever business I wanted, as long as I could show him I had a plan to see it through and make it profitable. I left his house that day calmer than I'd been in years."

"Why?" Sara asked.

"Because my mind was racing. I knew what I wanted to do."

Sara grinned. "The hardware store. How did Brian come into the picture?"

"He's much better with people than I am, so I approached him to co-own with me. A hardware store is a huge investment, and I knew Brian had a hefty inheritance from his grandparents. Plus, if Mr. Garrison only put up my half, I wouldn't feel so bad about taking him up on his offer."

"So, he just gave you the money?" There wasn't ac-

cusation in her voice. She'd already told Ian about how
Mr. Garrison had paid for her college education and
housing until she could support herself.

"Yeah, with one condition."

Sara skipped over to him and wrapped her hands
around his arm. "Spill it."

Ian was so distracted by Sara's playful affection that
he didn't answer right away. For a moment, he could
imagine her ten years younger without a care in the
world. What would she be like had he been able to give
her the life she deserved?

The wind blew a cold gust, and Ian tugged her
closer. "He said I had to do anything he asked."

"And you said yes? That's so vague. Did he ever ask
you to do anything?"

Sara's questions brought the past to the forefront.
"Not until recently."

Sara stilled. "How recently?"

"It was in my note," Ian admitted.

Sara whispered. "What did the note say?"

Ian turned to her and rubbed his hands over the
tops of her arms. She had to be getting cold. He wasn't
ready to tell her about the note yet, so he told her something else that she needed to know. "I'm sorry I didn't
tell you how I felt about you before... everything. I feel
like by not telling you, I just let you walk away. I always
wondered if you'd known how I felt if you'd have let me
come with you."

"Ian—"

"Let me finish." Ian cupped her face and continued.
"I don't like talking about those years without you because I spent too much time chasing the wrong dreams.
I knew where I was meant to be. I should've been beside
you. I wanted you, and it killed me that I couldn't
have it."

"I'm sor—"

"No, wait. Let me finish. I need to tell you everything—everything that matters." He paused and let his thumbs trail an arc over her cheeks. "I kept thinking life with you would've been perfect had you and I went for it all those years ago. I would've done anything to make you happy, and I'd have been my best self for it. But I missed it all. All those prayers went unanswered, so I stopped—"

"No, they didn't," Sara corrected. "Look. I'm here now."

Ian grinned. "You're right. I just had to be patient," he whispered. "You're always right. I shouldn't have given up hope."

"Now, we have everything. We can have it all. It just wasn't in our timing. It was in God's timing."

Ian nodded. "I understand now." He leaned his forehead against hers and whispered, "We can't stay here."

Sara's whisper was caught by the wind. "I know. I don't want to take you away from your home. Your family and friends are here."

Ian loved his brother and his niece and nephew. He cared about his parents and his friends, even if they pushed him out of his comfort zone. He'd miss them all. He'd miss the hardware store, but he knew Brian could buy him out.

But she was the one he needed, and nothing could replace that.

"What about your shelter?" Ian asked. "Didn't you want it to be here?"

Sara shrugged. "With that kind of money, I can hire people to oversee everything. I don't need to oversee it myself. The point is that the people in need have a place to go. I think that's what Mr. Garrison had in mind for this place. Sometimes, people need a chance to get back on their feet."

It made sense. The house was off the beaten path, and it was proving to be a good place for Sara to lay low.

"Did you know Mr. Garrison grew up in that house?" Sara asked.

"Really? How do you know that?"

"It was in my letter."

He wondered what else was in her letter, but it wasn't fair to ask until he was ready to tell her about the contents of his own note from Mr. Garrison.

Sara took a deep breath and sighed. "What if this never ends?"

"What if it does? You know I'll protect you from anything. I'm not afraid of a backwoods outlaw."

Sara swatted his chest, and Ian caught her wrist. He stopped and focused on the fragile wrist in his hand. He never thought he'd be close enough to his best friend to touch her, but here she was in the flesh, her blood pulsing beneath his fingertips.

Sara's eyes were heavy with sadness. She'd always felt the hurt of others too deeply. "You have a family, Ian. I didn't. I know what you're giving up."

Ian leaned in and sealed his lips against hers. Breathing her in, he moved his mouth with hers, sliding into place like one piece of a puzzle fitting into another. He needed one more assurance that she was real. He needed to feel her acceptance, her kindness, and all the things that made her a light in a world of darkness.

When he pulled back, he was sure his heart would combust. "What if I want you to be my new family? What if I loved you then, and I love you now, and I'll love you until the day I die? What if I promise to love and cherish you forever, before our family, and our friends, and God?"

It was a huge risk, but he'd skipped out on a big opportunity to tell her he loved her once. He wouldn't let her wonder any longer. She would always come first.

Ian slipped his arms from around her and pulled the ring from his pocket. His dad was friends with a local jewelry store owner. Ian had called the man after leaving

Tyler and Sissy's the night before and arranged to meet him at the store after working hours. When Ian had explained what he was looking for, the man had agreed to open up and show him around.

Sara gasped. He wasn't sure she was breathing. Finally, a lone word pushed from between her lips. "Ian."

He slid down onto his knee in the damp leaves by the river. "What if you married me before we leave here? I don't want you to ever question where I stand with you." He took her hand and placed it over his heart. "I'll always be beside you."

A tear slipped down her cheek. "Ian! Yes! A thousand times yes." She pulled him to his feet and wrapped her arms around his neck.

He buried his face in her neck and breathed in the smell of her hair. He felt a shift in his heart. All the hatred and pain of the past was breaking apart, making way for the love he felt for her.

Ian hadn't told her she'd inspired him to open his Bible last night. He hadn't told her he'd read the love chapter again, even though he knew what it said. He hadn't told her he'd fallen asleep praying for forgiveness and guidance. And he didn't tell her she was the answer to every prayer. He could feel a change in his heart, and he knew Sara was perceptive of things like that.

Sara

I'm engaged to Ian Hart.

Sara repeated the line in her mind throughout the rest of the day. It seemed like a dream. In fact, it *had* been a dream for most of her life. Ian had chosen to be by her side every moment he'd been given a chance, and she would be sharing her life with a partner who cherished her above all others.

Returning from the river with a fiancé and an engagement ring, Sara was on cloud nine.

Ian held her hand and turned to her as they approached the house. "I think I'm gonna start pulling the old boards from the back deck. In a little while, I'll run into town and grab some lumber for the repair and stop by my house for some clothes."

"I'll help pull boards. I'm not ready to go back inside. The paint smell was a bit much."

Ian squeezed her hand. "Sounds great. I have an extra crowbar in the truck."

Sara sat on the bottom step of the deck and leaned back on her elbows. Tilting her head to the sky, she let the lukewarm rays of sunshine rest on her face.

Ian was on the phone when he returned from his truck. "Yeah, that should do it. I'll be there around 6:00 this evening to pick it up. John and I can handle it."

Ian moved the phone from his ear and whispered, "Brian," letting her know who he was talking to. Ian listened to Brian for a moment before asking, "How are things in the office? You managing okay?" There was a pause before Ian said, "Good. Let me know if I need to swing by. Otherwise, you know where to find me."

When he ended the call, he showed her how to pry the boards up and where to stack them. They fell into a comfortable routine.

Sara timidly broke the peaceful silence. "So, I don't even know where you live."

A million thoughts raced through her mind with the revelation. She didn't know where her fiancé lived. If he was willing to leave here with her someday, he'd have to leave that home.

"My house is on this side of town. I can show you tonight if you want. I think the whole idea that you shouldn't leave the house was so you wouldn't be seen in town, right?"

Sara's heart raced. "Yeah, that's right."

"It's up to you."

She was afraid to see it. What if she loved it? She knew from experience that having to leave something she loved was hard.

But she wanted to see where Ian lived. It was a missing piece in the puzzle that formed the years she'd missed in his life. "Sure. I'd like to get out of here for a bit."

Ian's smile grew wide. How she'd missed that mark of joy. Seeing Ian happy was one of the best things in life. It hit her anew that she'd just agreed to marry him. She'd make it her mission to see him happy as often as possible. Ian had never slacked when it came to proving his devotion, and he deserved the same from her.

Sara bumped shoulders with him. "I love you."

"I love you too. Always have." Ian gave her a wink that stole her breath.

She repeated the words in her mind again. *I'm engaged to Ian Hart.*

Ian called Brian to let him know he would pick up the lumber the next morning. Ian didn't want to go into town with Sara in the truck. Instead, they waited until later in the evening and took backroads around the heart of town to get to Ian's house.

Sara watched out the dark window for a few miles. She couldn't discern much from only the headlights, but she didn't see anything she recognized from her childhood.

Finally, she turned to Ian and reached for his hand. "I wish I could see something. I only saw a little of downtown when I went to the meeting with Andrew."

Ian chuckled. "It looks the same. At least that was what I thought after coming home after the years with the marines."

"You haven't said much about your medical discharge. You said it was your foot?"

"Yeah. I broke a few of the bones in my foot, and it required surgery. The recovery was long, and I was discharged. I get it. I was a liability. I went in knowing the stipulations of the job. But back then, I was even more of a hothead, and being tied down for weeks made everything worse. Coming home to Julie's surprise and being back in the place that reminded me of you was tough. I gave everyone a hard time."

Sara leaned back. "You? Difficult? I can't imagine."

Ian lifted her hand and placed a kiss on the back. Her skin tingled where his lips had lingered, and she was consciously aware of the stunning ring a mere inch away from the spot of his affection.

Ian pointed out the turns for her. "I just want you to know how to get here in case you ever need to. Plus, I assume we might be able to live here for at least a little bit until we find another place wherever we end up. I think it's best to stay at Mr. Garrison's house for now, since we're still working on it. We'd be back and forth every day, and you should minimize your time on the road around here."

"Of course, it's fine with me if we stay there." They hadn't set a date for when they would be married, but while they were still working on the house, they'd have time to talk about it. They could finish up at Mr. Garrison's, get married, pack up Ian's house, and choose their next home.

Ian pulled into a driveway, and Sara sat up in her seat. Ian's house was a single-level house covered in varied brown brick. Sara squinted through the darkness to make out the swing on the porch. There weren't any neighbors close-by, and she wondered if he'd purposefully isolated himself.

Ian parked the truck in the garage and turned to her. "This is it."

Sara smiled. "I can't wait to see it."

"Wait here."

He rounded the truck and extended a hand to her as she stepped out. Holding her hand, he led her to the door and inside.

The house wasn't new, but it was well maintained. They stepped into a kitchen with distressed, slate-colored cabinets and a cream marbled countertop swirled with gray. The appliances were all top of the line, and the tile floor was spotless.

"This is the kitchen." He led her into a common room. "This is the living room."

Sara's heart constricted. She loved it. Everything about the place was calling to her. The colors were muted blues and grays—her favorite colors. The framing was crisp white lines, and the furniture was billowy and inviting.

Sara's voice broke as she nodded and said, "It looks like home."

She turned to him, and he opened his arms to her. He probably hadn't decorated the house himself, but everything around her screamed comfort and safety. Maybe the feeling came from Ian and not the structure itself.

He brushed his hand over her hair and whispered in her ear, "It's just a place. We can find another home you like."

"I haven't lived in a real house since I left Carson. Apartments were always easier, knowing I wouldn't be staying." She looked up at him. "I want you to have a home."

"You are my home." Ian brushed his hands through her hair and leaned in to kiss her temple. "You're all I need."

Sara whispered back, "And you're all I need."

Ian's strong arms wrapped around her, pulling her to him. She clung to him as the bond they'd kindled as kids solidified.

Ian's lips brushed across hers, and she felt his grip tighten on her waist. Gripping his back, she pulled him closer. It was as if his mouth, body, and mind knew the way of hers.

They would be one. She was meant to marry this man, to join lives and souls with him and create a family. The person who understood her—her best friend— would soon be her husband.

"I love you, Sara. A house or a job doesn't mean any- thing to me. We can live anywhere you want, wherever you feel safe. I'll find work. You have to know that you're not alone. You never were."

No, she wasn't alone. Her protector had come, and she was safe at home.

Sara

～

I an had thrown together a bag of clothes and
necessities before they left his house, locking it up
tight since he wasn't sure when he'd be back.

Mr. Garrison's house only had one bathroom, but
thankfully, Ian had quickly remodeled the parts needing
attention first. The new flooring was crisp and clean,
he'd replaced the shower head, and he'd even installed a
new toilet.

Sara showered first, while Ian put some of his things
away in his new bedroom.

When she was young, knowing Ian was close-by had
instilled calmness in her. Now, she felt safe, but her
emotions and senses were hyperaware of the handsome
man in the next room.

My fiancé, she thought. *He's my fiancé. He wants to
marry me.*

It still seemed surreal. Sara hadn't ever dated anyone
seriously enough to matter. She'd gone on dates with a
few boys in college, but there hadn't been hope for a future. How could she have told them she'd be living her
life looking over her shoulder? Who would be willing to
marry her and start a family knowing they might be
uprooted?

Ian Hart, that's who.

Sara dressed in her sweatpants and T-shirt and brushed through her wet hair. How would Ian react to seeing her like this? She wasn't typically self-conscious about her looks, but this was her most raw form.

If he was willing to marry her, he might as well know what he was getting into. She opened the door to find him sprawled on the couch. His arms hung over one end, while his bare feet dangled over the other. He wore a white T-shirt and gray sweatpants.

Sara smiled. She could be herself around him. He knew her heart, and he loved her for what he found inside.

The bathroom door creaked behind her, and Ian stirred. He rubbed his eyes and sat up. "The TV doesn't work."

She shrugged. "Sorry. I should have warned you to bring entertainment."

Ian stood and went to her. His mouth turned up in a grin, and his eyes danced in the muted lamp light. "You're so beautiful. I can't stop looking at you." He rubbed his calloused fingertips along her jaw. "I dreamed about you a lot, but you're prettier in person."

When his finger slipped from her chin, he sighed. "I want to kiss you, but I don't want to overstep any bounds. I want our wedding night to be special."

Sara smiled. Of course, Ian would dispel any notion she might have that he expected something physical to happen between them while they slept under the same roof. He'd always been her safe place, and nothing had changed.

"It *will* be special." She linked her fingers with both of his hands. "I'll be your wife. We'll be one for the rest of our lives."

Ian shook his head, keeping his gaze locked with hers. "I can't believe this is happening."

"Me either."

Ian leaned closer. "About that kiss?"

Sara chuckled. "You can kiss me, Mr. Hart."

She didn't have to tell him twice. His lips covered hers in the sweetest of kisses. His touch whispered his devotion, his respect, and his eagerness to forever be bound to her. It was slow but firm, and her head was spinning by the time he pulled away.

Ian closed his eyes and took a deep breath. "Okay, now what? What have you been doing without a TV or internet all this time?"

Sara wound her arms around his neck. "I've been crashing around 7:00 every night, but I usually read before bed."

"Snack and books. Got it."

She rolled her eyes with a smile. "I'll get you a snack." She was back a moment later with a bag of chips.

Ian sat on the couch and accepted the bag and said, "You don't have to get me anything. I'll figure out where things are."

"I know. I wanted to butter you up for my next request." She sat on the couch beside him and curled her legs under her.

"Should I be worried?" Ian asked.

"I read my Bible every night. Can I read to you?"

Ian spotted her Bible sitting on the end table and reached for it. "What if I read to you tonight?"

Sara's eyes widened. *What if he shocked her to the core?*

"I'd like that. The bookmark is where I stopped."

He pulled the marker and opened the book to 1 Corinthians Chapter 16. "Thank you for being past the love chapter." He grinned.

"What? Are you saying you don't need a reminder?" Sara asked.

"You're going to want that one read at our wedding, aren't you?"

Sara fell back onto the couch in a fit of laughter. "It's quite possible. Get ready to hear it again."

She rested her head on the throw pillow, and Ian tucked her feet into his lap, resting his hand on her leg as he began reading.

Sara let her eyes fall closed as she listened to Ian read God's word. She'd never been more comfortable than she was in this moment.

"Be watchful, stand firm in the faith, act like men, be strong. Let all that you do be done in love."

When he finished the chapter, he continued reading into 2 Corinthians Chapter 1. She listened as he read Paul's letter of God's comfort and drifted to sleep.

Sara

Sara woke to the sun streaming through her bedroom window the next morning. She stretched the aching muscles in her back and arms then listened. The house was quiet.

The extra blanket wasn't draped over her feet the way she normally slept. She sat up in the bed and remembered curling up on the couch the night before for Ian to read to her.

He must have carried her to bed. She'd been so tired from pulling boards and painting the day before, she hadn't woken. From the stillness of the house, he must still be asleep.

Her phone rang on the nightstand beside her. No one called her except Trisha, especially this early.

"Hello." Sara wiped her eyes and lay back onto the pillow.

"I thought you were going to call me when he left," Trisha said in greeting.

"I was. He didn't leave."

Trisha huffed. "Excuse me? Please tell me you're not saying what I think you're saying."

"I'm not, but I have so much to tell you. It's been a whirlwind."

A car door slammed on Trisha's end of the line. "Please start at the top."

"Well, about five minutes after I got off the phone with you, he told me he loved me." Sara ran her finger along the seam of the sheets. "He said he'd always loved me."

"Aww, I knew it! He's always carried a torch for you."

"Yeah, then he told me a little bit more about what went on with him during our time apart. He went through some hard times too."

Trisha sighed. "I can imagine. I don't even want to think about what it would be like to be separated from Paul now that I know what it's like to be with him."

"Exactly. He got married, but it didn't work out. Then he went in with his friend and opened a hardware store in town. It's doing really well."

"That's awesome. You're getting all cozy with the big boss."

Sara laughed. "Then, he proposed."

"He what?" Trisha squealed. "Hold the phone, I think I missed something. He asked you to marry him?"

"He did! He said he knew I probably couldn't stay here after this renovation, and he wanted to go wherever I go."

"What about his business?" Trisha asked.

"He said he thinks Brian will buy him out." There was a lot of hope and maybe hanging on that stipulation.

"Wow. Congratulations, friend! When's the wedding? Am I going to be able to make it?"

"I don't know. It'll probably be a courthouse affair. We can't exactly have a big to-do here in town while I'm hiding out. No one knows I'm here. Plus, I don't even have an internet connection here to plan anything."

"Yeah, I'm sorry. I know you'd want to be married in a church."

Sara bit the inside of her cheek and cleared her throat. "It's okay. Maybe one day we could renew our vows in a church."

"I wish I was there with you. I haven't seen you in years, and I feel like I'm missing so much."

"It's okay," Sara said. "You have a life on the other side of the world. I get it." Sara twirled the ring on her finger and studied it in the morning light. "Then he gave me this beautiful ring and he took me to see his house when it got dark."

"What's that like?" Trisha asked.

"His house is gorgeous. It feels like home."

"Oh, sweetie."

Sara sighed. Trisha knew her constant search for a home—a place that would last. "He said he wants to stay here with me now that he knows the stakes. I should have known he'd want to be closer. He's always been my first line of defense."

"How awkward was it?"

"Not at all," Sara said. "He was a perfect gentleman. He even read my nightly Bible study to me out loud. At least, he did for a while. I fell asleep and he carried me to bed."

"That sounds... cozy."

"Oh no," Sara corrected. "He has his own bedroom. He was sure to make it clear last night that there were boundaries here he would respect."

"How thoughtful of him," Trisha pointed out.

"Yeah, this is my first real relationship, and I'm engaged after like a day."

"Is it really that fast though? You've gone on and on about Ian Hart since the day we met. You already knew you wanted to be with him, and he wants to be with you. He sounds pretty devoted to me."

Sara sighed. "I just don't know what to do. I don't know how a serious relationship works."

Trisha scoffed. "Don't worry about that! It'll come.

Every relationship is different, and you and Ian are going to figure yours out together. Don't sweat it."

"Things are different for people like me and you. How did you make it work with Paul?"

"You mean with my baggage?" Trisha asked. "It took me a *long* time to tell him, but I'm glad I did. The key is trust and faith. You have to trust that God put the right man into your life."

"You're right. Ian is so good to me. I just can't believe we found each other again."

"Life is funny that way." Trisha yawned. "I gotta go. My bed calls."

"Love you, Trish."

"Love you, Say-Say. I hope I get to be the matron of honor at your wedding."

"Same."

Sara disconnected the call and heard Ian moving things around in the kitchen. He was probably making coffee.

She stretched her legs, and then jumped out of bed eager to see her fiancé.

Jan

The next few weeks passed in a blur of exhaustion. They were both eager to finish renovating the house and move on to the next chapter of their lives together. The sooner they tidied up Mr. Garrison's old house, the sooner he'd be kissing his bride and riding off into the sunset with her.

As excited as he was to be starting a lifelong relationship with Sara, the things they still had left to do weighed on them both. He needed to get his house on the market, and that might take a while. Not to mention, he still hadn't told any of his friends or family about his plans to leave with Sara.

A few of those conversations would be tough. His parents hadn't ever tried to strap him down, and they would understand why he had to go once he told them about Sara. Leaving his nieces and nephews would be hard, and his other friends had kids too. He wouldn't be here when Jake and Natalie's baby was born.

All those kids would grow up and forget him. He wouldn't be a regular part of their lives the way he was now.

How was he going to tell Brian about leaving the business? Sure, things were going well enough that

Brian might be more than willing to take over on his own, but they'd always balanced each other out and taken some of the load off the other. Brian had a growing family of his own, and shouldering the business might not be something he'd want to do.

Ian stepped into his house and looked around. He had so much to do before they could put the house on the market. Moving would be time-consuming. They could just donate most of it, and he'd be fine living a more minimalist lifestyle like Sara.

He'd only stopped by to check the mail and pay some bills, but he decided to get some things together and drop them by the donation center on his way to the hardware store. He told Brian he'd come by the office today and tie up some loose ends. Maybe he should break the news to Brian that he might be leaving soon.

He had a garbage bag half filled with T-shirts when his phone rang. He swiped to answer and stuck the phone between his shoulder and ear.

"Hey, Sis."

Sissy's usual peppy voice held a hint of panic. "Ian, what's going on?"

Ian stopped shoving shirts in the bag and looked up. "What are you talkin' about?"

"I was at the grocery store where Ms. Miller was telling *everyone* that Liz Jennings inherited a billion dollars from Mr. Garrison! I hadn't even heard the man had died or that Liz was back in town. Then, she went on to tell about how she heard that Liz's dad is in prison for kidnapping girls and that's why Liz left. Ian, what's going on? Is that where you've been these past few weeks?"

Ian's mouth went dry, and a cold chill raced down his spine. This was their worst nightmare come to life. He quickly asked, "What else did she say?"

"Nothing! I got upset that if all that was true, she

shouldn't be gossipin' about it, and I told her to shut her mouth and stop messin' in people's lives."

"Good." The blood pounded in his ears, and he fought to concentrate on the conversation. His mind was reeling with plans.

A car door slammed on Sissy's end of the line. "Is it true? If it is, you and Liz could be in danger. Kidnapping! Who all was involved?"

"It's a long story."

Sissy paused. "Not long enough. Ian, it's in the newspaper!"

"What?" Ian spat.

"I just grabbed yesterday's paper from the box. There's an article on the front page. *Local runaway inherits a billion dollars.* It has to be her."

"Yesterday. Everyone in town has read that article by now." Ian dropped the bag and scrubbed a hand over his head. "I have to go."

"Ian, let us help." Sissy's voice was shaky. "We're your family. We'll do anything for the two of you."

"I know, but you have kids, and I don't want them anywhere near this."

Sissy was quiet for one heartbeat before she whispered, "Okay."

"Thanks, Sis."

He hung up the call and dialed Sara's number as he stomped through the house to his truck. She didn't pick up until he was in the garage.

"Hey, how is everything at the house?"

Ian spoke quickly. "Everyone in town knows you're here. There's an article in the newspaper, and Sissy just called. She said Ms. Miller was talking about you at the grocery store."

"No! No, we've been so careful." Sara's deep breath huffed over the line. "She saw me that day. Ms. Miller was at Andrew's office the day we met with him. I wonder if Tracy said something. Are the probate court's records public?"

The panic he feared laced Sara's voice. He started the truck and backed out of the garage. Ian interrupted her rapid-fire questions. "Don't worry. I'm on my way now."

But when he backed out into the daylight, a white car was pulling into his driveway, blocking him in. "Someone's here. I need take care of this, and then I'll be right there."

"Wait, don't come here. Go to work like normal."

Right, he shouldn't lead anyone straight to her.

"Okay, but text me regularly until I get there. I'm coming."

Sara's voice was soft and reassuring when he was the one barreling into a full-on panic now. "I know. I'll be careful. Just do what you have to do."

"I love you," Ian said.

"I love you too."

He disconnected the call and stormed from the truck. He didn't have time for whatever they were selling.

A woman stepped from the passenger side of the car, and he knew who she was instantly. Regina Kirkpatrick was a reporter for Channel 15 News.

She was in her early fifties, but her skin was smoothed and doctored in unnatural ways. Her hair and makeup were flawless, and her smile beamed as if she were ready to kill with kindness. A man in a brown jacket rummaged in the backseat of the car.

"Hi, you must be Ian Hart. I'm Regina Kirkpatrick of Channel 15 News." She extended her slim hand to him as she approached. "Do you have a moment to answer some questions for me?"

Ian shook her hand and decided to be blunt with her. "Actually, I'm busy, and I won't be answering any questions. No need to stop back by."

Regina's smile didn't falter, as if she were used to breaking down walls. "Mr. Hart, I'm sure you're aware of the controversy surrounding Ms. Jennings and her inheritance. It's my understanding you were once close with Ms. Jennings. Is that true?"

"That sounds like a question to me. And I believe I've made it clear that we're finished here."

Regina tilted her head and held her pageant smile. "Yes, you did say that, but you should know that I'm not the only one who's been waiting for you to come home. Quite a few others are interested in expanding on the story of the kidnapping ring that was hushed up in this quiet little town twelve years ago. Do you blame them?"

"More questions." Ian stepped closer to Regina, but she didn't back down. He pointed to her car and sneered. "I think you need to get in your car and leave before I lose my temper. You're stickin' your nose where it don't belong, and I won't sit back while you put her in danger to get the next big story."

Regina's smile grew, and Ian's blood boiled. Having Sara in his life required that he master the anger he'd lived with for so long, but Regina was testing every weakness in his control.

"I think you just answered my questions, Mr. Hart. I'll be seeing you." She nodded and walked back to her car.

Ian stormed back to the truck and gunned it out of the driveway, as soon as the reporters were gone. He dialed Sara on his Bluetooth, unsure of where he was going.

"Hey," she answered on the first ring.

"It was a reporter. I'm not sure if she was bluffing, but she said there are more, and they've all been hanging around waiting for me to come home."

"They'll follow you, Ian. You can't come here. Go to work. Act like everything is normal."

"I get it, but I want to be with *you*." Ian scrubbed a hand over his head. His breathing was coming in ragged pants now. He needed to get to her. She needed him, but the last thing she needed was for him to lead anyone to her hiding place.

"I want you here too, but we'll have to make do. You showed me how to use the gun, and the security system is on."

He'd gone over the basics of how to use the semi-automatic shotgun over a week ago, and it had been propped against the back door ever since. "Do we need to go over how to use it again?" Ian checked his rearview mirror, and the white car was following him. He wondered if he could get Jake to do something about the reporters if they didn't back off.

"No, I remember. This is my life at stake. I take it seriously too. You forget that I did this on my own for years."

The media and the town busybodies couldn't hurt them, but he wondered how long it would take Owen McCall to get wind of this in Arkansas or wherever he was. Surely, he still had friends here sniffing around for any sign of the woman who used to be Liz Jennings. Kenny and Owen hadn't worked alone, and even Ian had heard of them back when. Bradford wasn't far from Carson, and everyone knew to avoid the McCalls. Ian had left Carson after graduation and hadn't noticed that the McCalls had gotten quiet.

"I know." Ian sighed. "That doesn't mean I want you going it alone now. It terrifies me." Losing Sara—again—would be too much.

"Mr. Garrison always kept everything about the trial and anything involved with the kidnapping ring quiet," Sara explained. "After the ringleaders were imprisoned, the town was safe, and he made sure I stayed safe too by keepin' it out of the news. He made up a story about me going to live with my grandparents, and he said he got word around town that my dad got a job on the northern border. He worked hard to keep this from starting a fire around here."

"There was so much we didn't know about him." Ian would give anything to have the old man back now. He wasn't doing as good of a job at protecting her as Mr. Garrison had done.

Sara sighed. "It's fine. We'll beat this. We just have to leave. Mr. Garrison would want that."

Pushing the timeline up was the best option they had. Ian could get Tyler to sell his house for him, and he'd settle things with Brian about the business on the road. His friend would never fault him for doing what he had to in order to protect Sara. He said a short prayer of thanks to God for sending Sara a guardian for so long.

"I'll go to the hardware store and let Brian know what's going on. He can tell Jake and see what he can do to keep the wolves off my tail. I'll go back home and get some things together and come to pick you up as soon as the coast is clear."

"Sounds good. I'll pack up here too."

She sounded so strong and determined. Her optimism wasn't shared by Ian.

"Call me every hour. I need to know you're all right. Call me if you see *anything* going on outside. I can be there in minutes. I'll have Jake on standby too."

"I'll call," Sara promised. "Just be careful. I love you."

He'd waited too many years to hear those words. Now, everything between them felt fragile and precious.

"I love you too."

Ian disconnected the call, feeling hollow and numb. He gripped the wheel as he drove and tapped his foot against the floorboard.

In a moment of clarity, he remembered to pray.

Heavenly Father, please protect her. I'm humbling

myself before You, and I need You. I can't do this on my own. Help us get through this and find a place we can be safe.

Sara needed a home, and he wanted to give her that peace more than anything.

Sara

ara's hand shook as she ended the call with Ian. How would he be able to get here to pick her up without leading someone to her?

She pushed the pad of her thumb into the edge of her top teeth as she looked around. What did she need to bring? This wasn't her first move, but she'd grown too attached to the small house that used to belong to her old friend.

Not knowing when she'd get to come back, she started packing clothes she didn't intend to wear anytime soon. Half an hour later, her phone rang, and she saw that it was Andrew.

"Hey, I should've called you," Sara said.

"I'm sorry. I've been out sick, and I just heard the news. I'm not sure how word got out, but I think the best course of action is to get out of town."

She pinched the bridge of her nose and closed her eyes. "I can't leave without Ian."

"So take him with you."

"He's being followed by reporters."

Andrew whispered a curse. "Can't you leave without him? You have a car. He could meet you somewhere."

She could, but how well would it sit with Ian if she left without him again?

"He would understand," Andrew confirmed.

"He would, but I don't want to do that unless I have to. No one knows exactly where I am yet. I have a little bit of time."

"Right," Andrew said. "I ran a search on Owen. He's still getting his mail in Arkansas, but I don't have his exact whereabouts."

"I get it."

"Mr. Garrison set aside a sizeable amount of money to be used in the event that you ever needed it. You have the funds to do anything necessary to get out."

"Thanks, Andrew. I'll keep that in mind."

"Check in with me sometimes. I need to know you're all right. I'll do everything I can to keep you safe, but I can't retract what's already been done."

"I know. You've been great. I'll check in."

Sara hung up the call and tiptoed through the kitchen and living room checking the windows and doors. The forest was quiet outside and still for as far as she could see.

Maybe it would all blow over. Who read the local newspaper these days anyway? *The Carson Corridor* was obsolete over a decade ago.

Zipping the gym bag of clothes she'd packed, she heaved it onto her shoulder and peeked outside the kitchen windows again before jogging out to her car and throwing the duffel in the trunk. If she had to leave on a dime, at least she'd be semi-prepared.

Her phone was ringing when she stepped back into the house. She locked the door and lunged for the phone. "Hello."

"It's me." Ian's deep voice was like a warm blanket wrapping around her shoulders. "I just talked to Brian and Jake. Brian is gonna come by your place in a little bit and stay for a while. At least until I can get there. No one is watching him. Jake and I have a plan to do some car switching and get anyone off my tail."

"Okay, I'm fine here. I just packed a bag and put it in the car in case I need to leave quick."

Ian was quiet for a moment. "I know you might need to leave before I can get there. Don't worry. We'll meet up soon. Just stay in touch and memorize my number."

"I already did. This isn't my first rodeo."

Ian chuckled. "I know. You're strong, and you can do this. You're just not alone this time. Even if I'm not right beside you, I'm with you through everything, and I'll get there as soon as it's safe for me to come to you."

Hearing Ian's tone relax and knowing he had faith in her was all she needed. They'd find each other again soon, hopefully tonight.

Sara asked, "What if this is the new car smell?"

She heard a door shut on Ian's side of the call just as he let out a booming laugh. "The what?"

"The new car smell," she repeated. "You know, when everything is great and new in the beginning, and then... it fades. What if this is too much for you after the new car smell is gone?"

"Are you talking about our relationship like an automobile purchase?" Ian asked with a chuckle. "I'm so much more attached to you than I am my truck."

At one time, she'd wanted a family. She still wanted that, but how could they have kids when Owen McCall might show up at any moment? Plus, she wasn't sure Ian wanted a family in conditions like this.

Sara whispered, "I just want the long run with you. I'm scared this is too much."

"Your life will never be too much for me to handle. I asked you to marry me because I want you to be my wife, now and forever. Not because I was unsure. I'm all in for the good times and the bad."

"We might not have the full married experience," Sara reminded him.

"It's okay if you don't want kids. I'd love to have a family with you, but I'd rather have you in my life than the whole nine yards with anyone else." Ian's tone softened. "If you ever decide you want a family, I know you'd be a great mother. I'd do anything to keep you all safe."

Tears stung Sara's eyes, and she squeezed them shut. She covered her mouth and nodded. He couldn't see her, but she couldn't gather her words yet.

Ian promised, "We're going to fight, together, to have the future we both want."

"I love you." Those three words meant more than the sentiment they described. They held the deepest, unfiltered emotions of her heart, and they were only meant for one man.

"I love you too. I want to pray for us."

She wasn't sure her heart could be fuller than in this moment. They were leading each other out of the dark, and with God on their side, no one on earth or elsewhere was a match for them.

Ian prayed, and Sara pulled the phone away from her mouth so he wouldn't hear her muffled sobs. They were happy tears, but she didn't want anything to make him question her resolve. She was bound to the man God had made just for her, and nothing could shake their vow.

Sara

ᢀ

Sara jumped from her seat at the kitchen table when she heard gravel crunching beneath tires. Hanging over the sink, she spotted a black Tahoe parking beside her car. It was Brian. She dumped the meager sandwich she'd been eating into the trash as she ran to the door.

Brian was stepping out of the truck. The sun was setting, but there was still ample light spilling into the clearing around the house. What if it wasn't Brian? He was much bigger than she remembered him being in high school, but she shoved the doubt to the side when she saw his face. She'd know that smile anywhere.

He bounded to the door to meet her. "Hey, Lizzy!" His excitement was short-lived as he remembered her name change. "Sorry, old habits." He turned to scan the area as he stepped to the door she held open for him.

"Don't worry about it. Get in here. Nobody followed you?"

"Nope. I've got stealth like a cheetah."

Sara chuckled. "I've missed you. It's good to see you haven't changed."

"That's me. Old reliable." Brian surveyed the small house and propped his hands on his hips. "Have you been sittin' around here in the quiet all day?"

"Pretty much. No TV and no internet."

Brian's eyes widened. "It's the Stone Age. I'm gonna grab my guitar out of the truck."

"That's a good idea."

When Brian returned, he locked the door behind him and laid the guitar on the couch. "Ian should be here in a few hours."

"Good. Can I make you some coffee? Have you eaten dinner?"

"I'll take a cup if it's not too much trouble."

Sara smiled. "I could use one myself." She wasn't planning to sleep until Ian showed up.

She passed Brian a cup of coffee before cradling her own in her hands. "You want anything in it?"

"No, ma'am. This is perfect." He closed his eyes as he took a deep breath and smelled the brew. "I haven't had a cup of coffee in weeks. Leah is pregnant again, and so is Lindsey. They all decided to ditch caffeine during the pregnancies, and I feel bad drinking it around them. I can't catch a break at work or at home."

Sara propped her elbows on the table and leaned closer. "Who are Leah and Lindsey?"

"Oh, Leah is my wife, and Lindsey used to be Lindsey Payne. She was in school with us."

Sara gasped. "I remember Lindsey!"

"She's Lindsey Calhoun now. She married Dakota a few years ago." Brian wiggled his eyebrows as he took another gulp of the hot coffee.

"Of course she is. Everyone knew those two would go the distance."

Brian shrugged. "She left for about six years, and Dakota didn't handle it too well. We almost lost him once."

Sara knew how close Dakota and Lindsey had been in high school. Sara could imagine what losing Lindsey would do to him.

Brian went on. "Dakota and Ian both had a tough

time dealing after the two of you left. Alcohol was Dakota's weapon of choice, and Ian defaulted to anger."

Sara slipped down in her chair. What she wouldn't give to take it back and change things.

Brian continued. "They're both better now. Even before you came back, Ian was *slowly* losing his sting."

"That's good to know."

"He missed you like crazy. It was hard knowing Mr. Garrison had these plans for the two of you and not being able to tell him."

Sara tilted her head and gave him a warm smile. "I appreciate everything you've done for us. Thanks for coming here tonight until Ian could get here."

"No problem. He'd have done the same for me if Leah needed help."

"Now, tell me about Leah."

Brian sat back, and his eyes lit up with his smile as he told Sara about his family. "Leah already had Emma when we met, and I'm pretty sure I owe Emma for softening her mom up to me. She was only four years old when we met. I adopted her later that year when we married. Michael is teething, and we have Caroline on the way."

"Your family sounds amazing."

"Leah will love you."

Sara's smile fell. "I wish I could get to know her. I wish I could meet everyone."

"You will one day," Brian said with resolve. "I've been prayin' that all this will go away so you and Ian can live a normal life. You've both been through a lot."

"It's fine. We'll manage." Maybe if she kept saying the words, they'd come true.

"I know. I'll keep prayin' though."

"Ian told me Jake's wife is pregnant too. That's good news for them." Her coffee had cooled, and she took a bigger gulp.

"Yep. They wanted to wait until they finished the

house they were building to have kids, and it worked out perfectly that things were getting tidied up when they got the good news."

"What about Declan King? Is he around?"

Brian nodded. "He joined the army for a while, but he's back on the hill where he always lived now. He got married a few years ago too. Her name is Addie, and you'll like her too. She was in a heap of trouble when she came to us too."

"Like what?" Sara asked.

"She was running from a violent ex-boyfriend. We took care of him." Brian winked at her.

"What do you mean?"

"Well, we all kept an eye on her and out for the guy, and when he came for her, we were ready."

Sara's blood pumped hard in her veins. "How? Who?"

"Me and the guys. We looked out for her and wouldn't let him get to her." Brian pulled the collar of his shirt to the side to expose a rippled scar on his shoulder.

Sara gasped. "Brian!"

"I got shot, and Declan got a blade, but Addie is safe now. She's not lookin' over her shoulder anymore."

Absorbing the enormity of the story he was telling her, Sara whispered, "I had no idea." What if there really was hope for a life without running?

"We look after our own. You're no exception."

Sara's heart swelled. "I know. Thank you for coming tonight and spending time away from your family to make sure I'm okay."

Brian crossed his arms over his chest and grinned. "We'll do the same for you. Addie didn't have to run, and you don't either." He took a gulp of his coffee. "Ian told me y'all want to leave. I get it, but I don't like it. I think we can handle this."

Brian seemed set in his belief that they should stay

and weather the storm, but maybe he didn't understand the gravity of the potential consequences of their inaction. She didn't want to bring the McCalls back to Carson. She knew what they were capable of back then, and it was best if they stayed away.

Standing, Sara gestured to a seat in the living room. "Let's hear a song."

Ian

Waiting for nightfall was torture. He'd packed the essentials and loaded them into his truck in the privacy of his garage, but he wanted to make sure no one was hanging around before leaving.

He'd called Tyler and Sissy first, and that phone call had been tough. He was happy to leave them to the task of explaining his absence to the kids. They would be devastated. Lydia adored Ian, and he'd appreciated being able to be himself around her. It was easy to relax and forget about the tougher parts of life around an innocent toddler.

The call had begun and ended with Sissy in tears, but there wasn't much he could do to change things. He and Sara needed to leave now, and waiting for the cover of darkness was almost too long. Owen McCall had at least a day's head start on them.

Next had been Ian's parents. His mom had shed some tears, but this wasn't the first time he'd warned them he intended to be gone for an indefinite amount of time. Coming from a marine family, his mom was used to good-bye.

His dad had held in the sentiments, but Ian could tell the old man was shaken. His dad knew the lengths

Ian would go to protect Sara, and the fight was coming to their door.

Ian sat on the edge of the bed and turned the phone over in his hands. There were people here he still needed to make amends with, and now, it was too late. His friends had stuck by him, despite everything he'd put them through, and he hadn't shown enough appreciation. Now, it felt hollow to cram in the apologies at the last minute.

Tapping the screen to dial Declan's number, he wondered if Addie would be close-by so he could do this once instead of twice.

"Hello," Declan answered. A baby screamed in the background.

"Hey, do you have a minute?"

"Sure." The noise receded, and Declan asked, "What's up?"

Ian sighed. "I'm leaving town tonight. I just wanted to say thanks for everything."

"Is this about Liz? I saw the article, but I didn't—"

"I know why you didn't call." No one wanted to poke the bear, and Ian was a grizzly. Especially when it came to Liz.

"I didn't know how you were taking the news." Declan huffed a sigh. "Remember how you helped us when Addie was in a similar situation? Well, we're always here if you need us."

Of course his friend would include Addie in their crusade. Ian would've done the same with Sara. The women Ian and Declan loved were tough as nails and not to be left at home cowering.

Ian rubbed his hand over his head and rested it on his neck. "Right. We were trying to keep it quiet, but the cat's out of the bag now. It's time to get her out of here. Everyone has families now, and we can't put them at risk."

"I get it. We'll be praying, but if you need a hand, just call. We'll come runnin'."

Years ago when Addie had been running from an ex-boyfriend, Ian hadn't been the most helpful friend. In the end, he'd come around and stepped up to help out. He'd been overwhelmed with grief back then, and his selfishness had kept him from being a better friend.

Now as he sat alone, wishing he could be with Sara when she needed him, he understood. Declan would have done anything to protect Addie, and Ian recognized that determination in himself. Declan had offered his help, but Ian was afraid he and Sara were beyond the point of staying and battling things out here.

"Thanks, man. I appreciate it. Is Addie around?"

"Yeah, I think she was just grabbing a bottle for Suzie."

A few seconds later, there was shuffling on the line and Addie said, "Hey, I'm here now. What's up? Declan has you on speaker."

"I just wanted to say good-bye," Ian said. "I need to leave tonight, and I won't be able to stop in before I go."

"Aww, Ian. I figured this was coming. Declan filled me in a little after we saw the article in the paper. Then Sissy explained the rest. I can't imagine what you're going through."

"Really?" Ian asked. "You lived it four years ago."

"Well, this isn't the same. I left and ended up where I was meant to be. Maybe that happens for the two of you, but I really wish your home could be here." Addie's voice cracked at the end and she sniffed. "Because we love you, and I know we'd love her too."

Ian pinched the bridge of his nose. He'd spent his whole life pushing people away, and now he was leaving when he finally wanted to stay. "I know, Addie. You'd love Sara. She's good down to her bones, just like you. Maybe we can figure out a way to stay in touch."

Addie sniffed again. "I hope so. We'll miss you, Ian. Take care of her."

"I will." He hung up the call before Addie started full-on wailing. The last thing he needed was to get her upset.

Ian glanced at the clock and tapped his heel on the floor. The red digital numbers on the alarm clock read 7:43 PM. Time was passing slower than molasses. He didn't feel comfortable heading toward Sara until the shops in town were all closed, but he could make his way to Jake and Natalie's and pass the time with them.

Ian didn't waste time on another pass through the house. There wasn't anything here that couldn't be replaced. He dialed Jake's number as he locked up.

Jake answered quickly. "Hey."

"Just letting you know I'm on my way. I should be there in about ten."

"All right. We're ready," Jake confirmed. "Marcus is here."

Marcus Channing was one of Ian's oldest friends and someone he could always call on if he needed a hand. Marcus and his wife, Tori, were the guardians of his four siblings ranging from thirteen to twenty-one years old.

It'd taken one phone call to Marcus. Ian's lifelong friend hadn't batted an eye when he'd explained he needed help tonight.

Ian drove the quiet streets of Carson, Georgia in a daze. Would he ever see these tree-covered roads again? Would they look different if he and Sara were able to come back here after another decade?

It didn't matter. He'd told Brian his plans to leave tonight, and his friend hadn't taken the news well. Brian was still hanging on to the hope that Ian and Sara would be able to stay and stand their ground. It wasn't a risk Ian was willing to take.

The problem was that the danger would never fully

pass, and living in the shadows wasn't a way to live. There were places where they could settle down and be free to go through life without looking over their shoulders every day.

Brian would understand one day. At least Ian hoped his friend could. Brian had been Ian's closest friend besides Sara his whole life, and severing that bond would be tough. Ian would have to protect Sara on his own. He wouldn't be able to fall back on Brian, Jake, Marcus, Dakota, or Declan anymore.

Ian had spent his life forming a strong loyalty to these men, and he trusted them with his life. Their friendship wasn't something that could be replicated.

Ian pulled into the driveway that led to Jake and Natalie's new house. They'd spent the last few years building their dream home on the outskirts of town. It wasn't gaudy or even large, but the house was custom built to their family's dreams.

The garage door was open, and Ian parked his truck in the bay next to Jake's silver truck. Marcus's car would be parked around back.

Ian was moving his packed bags over to Jake's truck when Natalie burst into the garage. Her face was shadowed by the bright light behind her.

She stood, paralyzed in the doorway, and her voice was shaky when she spoke. "Ian."

"It's okay. Everything is fine." Ian was sure of it. He intended to be careful tonight. More families than his depended on his discreet escape.

"Don't go." Natalie stepped from the doorway and launched herself at him. Tears poured down her cheeks, and her sobs weren't quiet anymore. "You can stay. We'll figure this out."

"I can't. It's best if we go before they come here looking." He'd feel much better if they were already on the road.

Natalie's voice was high and frantic. "Jake is a

deputy. They have the manpower now to help. If the McCalls come back, we can protect her."

Ian shook his head. "It's not that simple. I'm not willing to risk her or your family."

"I know. I would never suggest doing something that's dangerous for her, but can't you see? They're taking you away from all you have here. This is your home because *we* are here. We love you."

Ian would lose it if Natalie didn't stop. Didn't she see she was only making things harder? Leaving wasn't ideal, but he'd made a promise to Sara that he'd leave with her if that's what was best, and he intended to follow through. Sara was most important, and he wanted to be with her wherever she ended up.

Ian reached out his hand and laid it on Natalie's slim shoulder. "Sara is my home now. You're my friends, and that means more to me than you know." He squeezed her shoulder, and she whimpered. "But Sara needs me. We want to get married and live someplace where we don't have to hide."

Natalie nodded before tucking her chin in another fit of sobs.

Ian lifted his head to see Jake stepping up behind Natalie. Jake wrapped his arms around his wife and brushed a hand over her hair.

"It'll be okay. This is good for them," Jake assured her.

She turned to her husband and buried her head in his chest. Jake nodded once at Ian before leading Natalie back inside. Ian finished moving his bags to Jake's truck and went inside.

Marcus and Tori sat at the table with Dakota and Lindsey. Lindsey stood and wrapped Ian in a hug, hiding her face and the tears on her cheeks. "You weren't the worst boss."

Ian huffed and wrapped her in a hug. Lindsey had put up with more from him than most. He'd known her most of his life, and that meant more years he'd been a jerk to her.

"You'll be fine. I need you to be strong enough to help Brian through this. He isn't taking it well."

Lindsey wiped her face with the back of her hand. "I can imagine he isn't."

"Yeah, I assume he'll land a few punches before he accepts it."

Lindsey tried to laugh through her tears. "Any chance I could sneak one of those punches in for myself?"

Ian laughed with her for a moment before her giggles turned into uninhibited sobs. Dakota hugged her, and Ian stepped back.

Marcus was a man of few words, and Tori was tough as nails. Ian was shocked to see Tori's lip quivering.

Ian stepped up to Marcus. "Thanks for helping tonight."

Marcus nodded. "Anytime." He extended a hand to Ian. "We're always a call away."

Ian gave his friend's hand a firm shake. "Take care."

Everyone went to the vehicles they'd been assigned when they'd planned the scheme earlier. Ian was in Jake's truck, Marcus would take Ian's truck, Jake would take Marcus's car, and Dakota would stay with Lindsey and Natalie.

With almost a dozen good-byes in one night, Ian was feeling worn down and ready to see Sara. Good-byes reminded him of losing her, and he remembered that feeling all too well.

Sara

◦~◦

Sara listened to Brian playing the guitar as he neared the end of another song. With her head resting back on the couch and her eyes closed, she had almost calmed herself enough to forget about the threat she still faced.

Brian stilled the strings. "Another?"

"Sure. Keep playing as long as you want. I love your songs." She'd picked up her Bible once tonight, but her mind was racing too fast to concentrate on the words. Instead, she found she could pray silently while Brian sang.

In the quiet stretch of space before Brian began the next song, she heard footsteps. The faint rustle came from the front of the house. Raising her head and turning toward the door in the kitchen, she whispered, "Is that Ian?"

Brian had stilled, and he was watching the door too. "I don't think so," he whispered back. "He'd be more deliberate."

Sara turned to Brian, hoping he could communicate with her quietly enough to form a quick plan.

Brian raised a finger to his lips and rested the guitar on the floor without making a sound. While he was bent, he lifted the leg of his jeans to reveal an ankle holster and the gun it held. Slipping the gun from its resting place, he pointed toward the shotgun that rested against the back door.

Her gun was in the bedroom, but the shotgun had a better chance of hitting a target. She was shaking enough from the adrenaline pumping through her veins to know she wouldn't be a good shot right now.

The thought of using the weapon had bile rising in her throat. After seeing Brian's scar earlier, she was keenly aware of the impact a bullet could make. Brian had been lucky.

When it came down to her and Brian or whoever stood on the other side of that door, she knew she'd have to make the decision to choose herself and the one helping to defend her.

She eased to standing from the couch and held her breath as every step she took on the old wooden floors sent a creak echoing through the house.

Brian was moving toward the kitchen door when a sledgehammer burst through the particleboard it was made of. With one jerk, the hammer yanked the door-knob out, and the remainder of the door burst open, banging against the kitchen wall.

Raising the gun to eye level, Brian aimed at the first man who entered and fired. The ear-splitting boom filled the space that had been silent only seconds before. The man had been moving too fast for Brian to aim, and the shot missed him by inches.

With their element of surprise thwarted, Brian quickly aimed again, but a second man rushed in and dove for Brian's legs, wrapping them in a hold she'd only seen in football games.

The man grappling with Brian on the floor was a stranger. In the bits and pieces she could see of him, she knew the face was one she didn't recognize.

The other man—the one rising from the shock of

the bullet that had missed him by a hairbreadth—was Owen McCall.

Sara lunged the remaining step and grabbed the semi-automatic shotgun resting against the wall. Her shaking hands fumbled with the feeder, but she couldn't dislodge the shot.

She looked up, frantic for any scrap of extra time as she fought with the weapon. This had happened twice in her training with Ian, and he'd been the one to dislodge the jam. She watched as Owen lifted the heavy sledgehammer over his head where he stood towering over Brian and the man on the floor.

"No!" She screamed the word before Owen let the hammer fly. With that instinctual cry, she'd possibly saved her friend's life.

But now, Owen was looking at her, and Brian wasn't his target anymore.

"Run! Sara, just run!" Brian screamed as the man holding him down tried to pry the gun from his hands.

Sara yanked at the lever on the gun once more and gritted her teeth with the effort.

"I said run!" Brian yelled again, and she shoved the gun away and bounded out the back door.

Running from the light of the room into the night had Sara squinting to adjust to the darkness. Relying on what she knew about the back porch Ian had rebuilt, she bounded for the stairs, reaching for where the railing should be.

At the bottom of the stairs, she stopped when a gleam of metal caught her eye. A crowbar sat hanging off the edge of the decking, and she grabbed it. *Better to be armed with something than nothing at all.*

Owen was only a few steps behind her, and she hoped she could make it far enough into the pitch black of the woods before he caught up to her. Her only advantage was knowing the terrain. She knew where she was going, and Owen didn't.

Sara's gaze darted from the ground to the forest ahead and back to her bare feet. The sticks jabbed into her soles, but she didn't let herself limp or give the pain an ounce of attention. Pumping her arms, she ran, knowing this was life or death. If she died out here in the woods tonight, there was a chance no one would know what happened to her. Owen could take her anywhere after he killed her.

Mouth open, Sara panted for the air she needed to keep sprinting. She felt the cold sting of a tear beside her eye. Ian would be crushed if she was killed here tonight or taken without a trace. He'd never stop. He'd spend his life looking for her. That man hadn't once given up on her, and she knew his life would be filled with more heartache.

No, Ian would find her. Even if he came too late, he wouldn't rest until he found her.

She bounded over a bolder and landed hard on the broken end of a log. Her ankle turned, and she collapsed into the damp leaves.

Owen was racing up behind her, and she scrambled to right herself.

It was too late. Owen jumped over the boulder and descended on her.

Sara gripped the crowbar in her hand and swung as hard as she could toward him. It was dark enough that she wasn't sure where she was aiming, but she heard the sickening thump as the bar hit his skin. Owen screamed, and she took advantage of the surprise she'd wielded to scurry to her feet and keep running.

She ran until the rush of the water was close enough that she couldn't tell if Owen was behind her. There had been three days of heavy rain in the last week, and the river was hugging the top of the bank. The water rushed over rocks and fallen trees loud enough that it sounded like a waterfall with a bounding train inside.

Sara ran to the edge and stopped quickly. Turning

around, she scanned the area for Owen. He could be anywhere, now that she couldn't hear him. The faint moonlight shone through the winding gap in the forest at the river, but it wasn't enough to locate her pursuer.

Turning back to the flowing river, she contemplated her options. Could she cross it? The water was rushing, and she doubted she could fight the current without losing her grip and being swept downriver.

Sara listened again as her pounding heart rivaled the raging waters. Where was he?

Just then, Owen burst from the dark forest. Taken aback, Sara grabbed both ends of the crowbar and lifted it in front of her in defense. Owen barreled right into her, undeterred by the meager weapon she wielded.

The air rushed from her lungs as he collided with her. There was one second where time seemed to pass slowly. The moment when she hung in the air above the water with Owen McCall wrapped around her, dragging her to a cold, wet grave.

Sara's lungs screamed for air and her body was stung by millions of shards of ice as she plunged into the freezing water.

Ian

Ian focused on the patch of road illuminated by his headlights. There were only a few more minutes left until he'd see Sara again. Ian tried to tell himself he could be patient just as his foot fell heavier on the accelerator.

He was bounding up the quiet road leading to Mr. Garrison's old house when the light leading him shone on an old car parked by the mailbox at the end of the long driveway.

Ian knew something was wrong as he gunned it for the car, desperate to get a closer look.

No, he couldn't see a reason for a car to be parked at the end of the driveway, other than the need for stealth. They must have followed Brian here earlier.

Ian jerked the wheel to race up the winding gravel road. Jake's truck revved deep as Ian bounced over the rutted-out lane.

Ian had to believe he wasn't too late. The consequences of even the slightest delay were unbearable. Blood pumped hard through his veins, spurring him on, begging him to run to her.

He called Jake, ready to summon the guard into action.

"What's wrong?" Jake had a sense for trouble.

"Get over here and bring backup. Everything you have. There's a car here, and I don't know where they are yet."

"I'm on it."

Ian disconnected the call and dialed Sara's phone. He let the sound of the rings fill the car and threaten to choke the life out of him. The call was still ringing when he came to a screeching halt in front of the house. The door was open, and that was enough proof. Ian jumped from the truck and grabbed the gun at his hip.

Inside, he found Brian wrestling with a man he didn't recognize. The man bounded toward something behind Brian, and Ian spotted a gun and a sledge-hammer in the corner.

Brian and the man were too close to give Ian any opportunity to shoot, but he didn't need a bullet to take the man out. Brian had the man's head locked in a standing guillotine hold, and Ian took the opportunity to grab the weapons.

Within seconds, Brian had the man unconscious.

Ian scanned the room as his friend panted for breath. When he found no sign of Sara, he screamed, "Where is she?"

Brian pointed toward the open back door. "Hurry."

Ian yelled over his shoulder to Brian, "Stay here and wait for Jake. Tell him where to find us." He didn't wait to find out if Brian listened.

There was only one place she would go if she ran this way. His stride was long and quick as he bounded down the hill toward the river. Now was the time to pray. Ian prayed with all the faith he'd been missing in the years he'd turned his back on God. He prayed with every step.

Please let her be okay. Please let me make it in time. Please give her strength. Please don't let him take her.

Pleading and praying, he rushed down the hill as fast as his feet would carry him. He followed the same path he and Sara had taken when he'd asked her to be his wife.

He could hear the rushing water long before he saw the river, and he refused to accept the possibility. The river was high and fierce after the recent rains, and the water was unrelenting.

Please don't. God, please don't let her be in the water.

He reached the bank and squinted to see in the darkness. He couldn't hear her over the rapids, and he didn't see any sign of movement on the bank. Panic swept through him like a cold wind when he didn't see her.

Maybe she was farther downstream. Maybe she'd gotten off track and ended up at a different part of the bank.

Maybe she's all right.

His mind was grasping at any scenario that didn't involve her drowning in the freezing river alone. How could he have left her even for a moment? Why hadn't he insisted that she leave earlier today? Why hadn't he asked Brian to get her away from here?

He moved down the river, scanning the water and the bank as he went. Minutes passed without sign of her. Could she be farther up the river?

He was about to backtrack and check the area he'd already scanned when he spotted her. A fallen tree lay across the river, and Sara clung to a branch.

Ian raced to the bank nearest the tree and climbed on, hugging the trunk as he moved across it and closer to her.

He watched her clinging to the branch and extended his arm to her. He was still a few inches too far.

Just then, she released one arm and stretched toward him. She held out her arm, reaching for him. Ian wrapped his legs around the tree beneath him as he reached for her. Once he felt secure, he was able to hold on with his legs and reach for her arm with the other hand. Pulling her toward him, he yelled, "Let go! I've got you."

Sara squeezed her eyes closed once before letting go and focusing on him. He felt her weight settle in his grip, and he heaved her up to him. There wasn't a chance he'd let her go. He was holding on with everything he had.

Seconds later, Ian wrapped her in his arms. Still clinging to the tree beneath them, he held her to him and vowed never to let go. Her clothes were drenched, and she shook from the cold.

"Can you hang onto my back? I need to get us off the tree," Ian yelled to be heard above the roaring water.

Sara nodded, and Ian turned so she could grab on. Balancing on the trunk of the tree, Ian slowly moved them toward the safety of the bank.

When his feet hit the ground, he crouched to let her climb down from his back. She landed in a heap on the wet dirt and stumbled as she attempted to regain her footing.

"Wait, let me help." Ian's jacket was almost soaked now, but he shoved it from his shoulders and wrapped it around her before cradling her in his arms. Standing, he began walking upriver. "We need to get you closer to the house so they can find us."

"Who?" Sara's voice shook with her question.

"Jake is on his way, and he has backup coming." Ian was running now, trying not to jostle her, but desperate to get her closer to the medical attention she needed.

"I—I can't believe you found me." Sara sobbed, and her entire body was shaking more violently by the second.

"Of course I found you. I can't believe we got separated in the first place." He pulled her closer, desperate to warm her body with his own.

Ian had spent a lot of time talking to God lately, and there was one thing he was sure of now. The Lord had

Sara in mind when He created Ian, and He knew this woman would need someone to stand by her through anything. God knew Sara needed a determined man, one who wouldn't be afraid to run into the fire for her, and He'd made Ian to be that man for her.

Ian's mission in life had always involved Sara. He'd led her to church when they were kids, he'd given her a safe place when they were teenagers, and he'd protected her whenever she needed him. Through it all, her patience with him was meant to calm the fire inside him and help him learn to wait on the Lord. The best things in life were certainly worth waiting for, and Ian knew that now.

About halfway up the hill, Ian spotted half a dozen flashlights and recognized Jake's voice calling Sara's name.

"We're here, Jake!" Ian yelled into the dark night.

The lights turned toward them, and Ian ran to meet the search party.

Jake bounded up to them at the head of the group. "What does she need? We have paramedics here."

A few men shoved the bags they carried from their shoulder and began opening them.

Ian didn't release his hold on Sara as he panted. "She fell in the river. I don't know about any other injuries, but she needs to get warm. I can carry her back to the house."

Jake pointed toward the top of the hill. "Lead the way."

Ian continued his run. When he could see the lights of the house come into view, he leaned down to whisper to Sara, "Almost there. You're gonna be okay."

He believed the words. He knew them in the deepest part of his heart to be true. There wasn't another option. Sara had to be okay.

Sara

Cold.

Sara couldn't think of anything beyond the cold.

Her body shook, and her teeth clicked together as she fought to regain an ember of warmth.

Ian burst into the house and laid her on the couch before backing away. She felt the loss of his heat, and the freezing renewed.

People descended on her, and they worked like bees in a hive—constantly moving, but never bumping into each other or stumbling. They were pulling at her clothes, but she couldn't dislodge her arms from where they were wrapped up in Ian's jacket.

She heard questions every so often, but she couldn't answer. The shaking was too violent to override.

A few of the men lifted her onto a gurney. Ian was beside her as they moved her outside and into the ambulance.

Ian ducked his head low to follow the paramedic into the ambulance. He sat close enough that he could lay his hand on her leg, but he gave the man enough room to help her.

After all the wet clothes were gone, warm blankets

were piled on top of her, and Ian spoke to her in soft words as the paramedic checked her vitals.

She only caught a few of Ian's words. He said "I love you" enough that she heard that part. The rest was in bits and pieces. She forced her mind to concentrate on the here and now.

"Brian is okay," she heard Ian say. "He's banged up, but he was able to restrain the man that attacked him until the deputies could arrive. I didn't catch the man's name before they took him away."

Sara hadn't known that man's name either. He was likely one of the McCalls who hadn't been connected to the crimes twelve years ago. He might've been too young to be involved back then.

The ride to the hospital seemed to drag. Sara lay with her eyes closed, listening to Ian's voice to ground her to reality. If she focused on his words, she could block out the pain.

At the hospital, Ian stayed close as they moved her into a room. A doctor entered the room minutes later to examine her. Most of her body was numb, so she hadn't been able to tell the paramedics about any injuries.

After the exam, a nurse changed the fluids for Sara's IV and placed an oxygen mask over her face. With the warmth of the blankets seeping into her limbs, Sara was beginning to relax when Ian walked in.

She was happy to see him—so happy that her smile seemed to split her face.

Ian sat in the chair beside her bed and wrapped her hand in his. "The doctor said he thinks you'll be fine. It just might take some time to feel better. You have some bruises on your ribs, and he ordered some x-rays to see if anything is broken."

Sara nodded, but the movement was weak.

"Rest," Ian said. "I'll be right here. I'm not going anywhere. They'll be in soon to take you for x-rays."

With Ian beside her, she knew she was safe. Her body was exhausted, and she fell asleep.

When morning came, so did the visitors. The doctor had just approved her release, and Ian reached for her hand with a smile on his face. "You ready to go?"

"We still have to wait for the official discharge," Sara reminded him.

Brian and Jake walked in, and Sara sat up in the bed. The nurse hadn't been by since word came of her release, and she was still hooked up to the IV. She scanned them both for injuries. Brian had a bruise blooming on his cheek.

"Are you okay?" Sara asked him.

Brian waved her off. "I'm fine. Just a bruise. Although, I'm gettin' too old for this. I'll be sore tomorrow."

Jake chuckled and clapped a hand on Brian's shoulder. "Suck it up, buttercup."

Sara turned her attention to Jake. "What about you?"

Jake shook his head. "I'm all right." His phone rang, and he stepped outside to take the call.

Tyler walked in dressed in khaki slacks and a pale-blue button-up shirt. He smiled at Sara. "Hey, Lizzy. Long time."

She didn't correct his use of her old name. Tyler would come to know her as Sara in his own time, and it was nice being reminded of the good times they'd shared.

He was taller than the last time she'd seen him, and his lean build had grown toned instead of lanky. She'd been sixteen when he'd gone off to college. Tyler had been her neighbor too growing up, but he'd been older and much too interested in his studies to pay much attention to the girl down the street. Still, he'd been kind to her, and they'd always gotten along well.

"Ty! It's been way too long." Sara opened her arms, and Tyler wrapped her in a gentle hug.

Jake stepped back into the room and greeted Tyler before turning to Sara. "The girls said they wanted to come see you, but when I told them you were being released, they were more than happy to wait until you got home to visit."

Sara's mind swirled. "The girls?" A louder thought rang in her head. *Home?*

"Yeah, Natalie, Lindsey, Tori, and Addie are at my house. They were planning to ride together, and Leah was planning to watch the kids. Now, they'll just wait until you're discharged."

Tyler pulled his phone from his pocket. "Sissy told me to tell you she'd have to wait for Barbara to get there to watch the kids before she could get down here. I guess I need to call her and let her know she doesn't have to rush."

Sara hadn't even met some of the people who had spent their morning planning to come visit her. Her hospital room was already crowded with friends. How had her lonely life expanded so much in the last few weeks?

Sara rested her hand over her mouth to hide her quivering chin. "That's so sweet of them. They don't have to do that. I don't want to inconvenience anyone. I'm fine."

Jake laughed, and Brian shook his head.

Tyler explained. "These women have been talking about you since they heard your name. They're chomping at the bit to meet you."

"I'm sure they're interested in the big story," Sara assumed.

Brian's eyebrow shot up. "Nah. They know about

the McCalls by now. They're dying to meet the woman who tamed Ian."

Sara turned to Ian to gauge his reaction. He merely shrugged without unfolding his arms where they were crossed over his chest.

"I didn't tame him," Sara corrected.

Brian shook his head. "Ian hasn't insulted anyone in weeks. The town is in your debt."

Sara giggled and said in a kissy voice, "My grumpy bear is learning to play well with others."

Tyler said, "I don't know what you did, but we appreciate it."

Ian rolled his eyes just as the nurse walked in.

"Okay, everyone out. The patient needs some privacy to get dressed."

Sara's eyes grew wide. "Oh, I don't have clothes. I think they cut the ones I was wearing off me."

Jake snapped his fingers. "That's what I forgot. Natalie sent you clothes, but I left them in the car. I'll be right back."

Sara said her good-byes to Tyler and Brian before Jake returned with her clothes.

"Thanks, Jake."

"No problem," he replied. "I hope you get to feeling better, now that all this is over."

"Is it over?" Sara asked. "Did you find Owen? Did you arrest him?"

Jake's gaze drifted to Ian, but neither of them spoke for a moment.

Finally, Jake said, "We found Owen farther downstream. By the time we got him out, it was too late."

Sara focused on breathing. In and out. Owen had drowned in the river, and that could've easily been her fate. She wasn't ready to hear about death this morning, and the ache rose up in her chest.

"And the other man?"

"His name is Kain McCall. He's in custody. As far as we know, there aren't any more McCalls left."

Sara released a breath she'd held. *Focus. In and out.* "So, no one else is left to look for me? At least until Kenny is released?" Her dad might come for her, but it wasn't something she ever wanted to think about.

"Actually, Kenny isn't long for this world," Jake said. "Kidney failure is killing him. Your dad isn't doing too well either. His age is catching up to him."

It was all too much to process and so morbid. Death had come like a thief in the night for the McCall family.

Jake scratched the back of his head and handed Sara the bag. "I told Natalie you were about her size and she sent something comfortable. I'm guessing you're going straight home."

Sara turned to Ian. "Um, where is home? Should I go back to Mr. Garrison's house?"

Jake answered, "Mr. Garrison's house is still a wreck. It needs a new door for sure." He tipped his imaginary hat at them. "I'll see y'all later. I'm sure Natalie and I will be swinging by soon." He winked at Sara. "Stay safe."

When they were alone in the room, Sara turned to Ian. He was already moving to sit beside her on the bed.

She slowly threaded her fingers between his. Focusing on their linked hands, she asked, "Where do I go from here?"

She was free to do whatever she wished and go wherever she wanted to go for the first time in her life. Who knew the freedom would pose so many questions?

"We didn't get a chance to get married before everything happened. If you want, we can do that now."

Sara hesitated. "We could…"

"Or," Ian offered, "we could take our time and plan a nice wedding."

Sara smiled. "It's not that I want anything fancy. The wedding isn't the best part about marrying you. It's just that today I realized that you have friends, and I want them to be my friends too. I think it would be really great to have a small wedding where we celebrate our marriage with our friends and family."

Ian nodded. "That sounds perfect. How soon can we make that happen?"

Sara laughed. It was flattering that he was so eager to marry her. "Maybe a month."

"I really don't want you going back to Mr. Garrison's place. If you still want to make the repairs and use it for your shelter, I can get Declan and Dakota to work on it. They own a construction company." Ian rubbed his hand over the short, rough hairs on his head. "And I'm guessing you don't want to live with me until after we're married."

Sara nodded. Staying at the same place with him had been a matter of her safety before, but the threat was gone now. "I'd like to move in when I'm your wife." She wrapped his hand in both of hers and squeezed. She'd miss their nightly Bible reading. The time they spent in prayer and reading together was special to her.

"I have an idea," Ian said.

"What's that?"

"Declan has a house on the farm that his grandparents lived in before they died. Addie lived there for a while before she and Declan were married, and Natalie lived there too. I think it's empty right now. You could move most of your things into my place and just take some necessities with you to stay there."

Sara's smile grew. "Yeah? You think he'd let me rent it for a few weeks?"

"I bet he would. And Addie would be close-by and could help you with wedding plans. She's a hopeless romantic."

"I can't wait to meet her."

Ian picked up the bag of clothes and handed it to

her. "Let's get you out of here. Sissy is probably waiting in my driveway to meet you."

Ian leaned down and kissed her sweetly, lingering and assuring her that he was ready for what the future held for them. He would be patient, and he'd give her the wedding she'd always dreamed of surrounded by their family and friends who loved them.

Sara grabbed the bag as Ian left the room. With the bruising and sore muscles slowing her down, she couldn't get dressed fast enough. Ian's friends were eager to meet her, and she wouldn't make them wait.

Ian

Ian parked the truck and killed the engine. He didn't rush to get out. Sara unbuckled her seatbelt and scooted across the seat of the truck. The cab light cast a blinding brightness on her face, and his attention was glued to her smile. She wrapped her hands around his upper arm and rested her head on his shoulder.

He didn't speak. He kissed the top of her head as the light dimmed, and tapped his finger on the top of her hand three times.

She tapped back once. She always tapped once, letting him know she was okay.

Ian whispered into her hair, "We don't have to go in if you're not ready."

Sara nuzzled closer. "I've been waiting for this moment for a while. I think *you* might be the one with reservations."

A month ago, he would've dragged his feet into Rusty's to meet his friends for one of their big revelation get-togethers. Now, things were different. He was different, and Sara was beside him.

"I'm ready," Ian said. "We're finally celebrating something I had a part in—something I can be proud of."

"You weren't proud of your friends?" she whispered in the dark truck.

"I was, but I was also bitter and jealous... and missing a big part of myself."

Sara playfully shoved his shoulder with hers. "Let's go."

Ian stepped from the truck, and Sara scooted the rest of the way to his side. He lifted a hand to help her out, and she took it, squeezing hard.

He liked it when she intensified small assurances like holding hands. It let him know this wasn't a dream. Sara was here, and she was happy to be holding his hand.

Ian rested his hand on the door leading into the restaurant and turned to her. "Last chance to run."

Sara swatted his arm. "Get in there!"

Ian chuckled and opened the door, moving aside for her to enter first.

The entire side of the restaurant facing the stage was filled with their friends and family. The group's laughter muted when they caught sight of Ian and Sara walking in.

Sissy jumped from her seat with baby Jace on her hip and ran to greet Sara with a smile. Sara opened her arms and wrapped them both in a hug.

"We're just waiting on Jake and Natalie. She's having morning sickness... all day," Sissy explained.

"That's awful. I hope it gets better soon," Sara said.

Sissy shrugged and turned to Jace. "The struggle is worth the reward."

Ian's heart lurched. He would endure every struggle again to be here tonight with Sara and his friends, but he knew he'd one day do anything to protect and provide the best life for the family he intended to build with Sara.

Sara caressed baby Jace's cheek, and he reached for her hand. "I have no doubt." It had been a week since Sara was released from the hospital, and she'd spent most of her time with her new friends and their families.

Jake's booming voice shouted behind them, "We're here! Let's get the party started."

Sara pulled Natalie in for a hug, and Sissy began jumping on her toes.

"Tell us! Tell us!" Sissy's excitement was infectious.

Sara looked up at Ian, and he pulled her in close to his side. He'd never been prouder than in this moment. He was surrounded by a group of amazing friends, and Sara was looking at him as if he'd hung the moon.

"You do it," Ian whispered.

Sara turned to her friends and shouted, "We set a date!"

Sissy screamed, and Jace cried. "I knew it! I'm getting another sister!"

Sara began to sob as she wrapped Sissy and Jace in a hug.

Ian watched his bride-to-be and marveled at her radiance. She was bursting with happiness, and he'd get to spend the rest of his life beside the woman who loved him as much as he loved her.

Jake clapped a heavy hand on Ian's back and said, "Congratulations, man. It's about time."

"Thanks." Ian's throat was tightening up, and he didn't trust himself to say much more.

The women flocked to Sara, and she was quickly wrapped in a huddle of happiness.

"Do you have a dress?" Lindsey asked. "When's the wedding?"

"Yeah," Natalie sighed. "Do I need to be shopping for a maternity dress?" She hadn't begun showing yet, but she would in the next few months.

Sara smiled and grabbed Natalie's hands. "We're aiming for the beginning of next month. No need for a maternity dress." She turned to the rest of her friends and said, "We want something small at the church. Just close friends and family."

The guest list is in this room, Ian thought. Even his parents were milling close-by accepting congratulations. The only people missing were Sara's friend, Trisha, and her husband, Paul. They'd be flying in from Paris the day before the wedding.

"Can I help you plan?" Addie asked. "I love weddings."

"Of course," Sara said. "I can come by in the evenings. I need your input on the Carson Mission too."

Andrew had come by the day of Sara's release from the hospital to let her know he was releasing Mr. Garrison's account with the promised funds of one billion dollars to her. It would take some time to approve through the court, but the funding she needed to start the non-profit that meant so much to her was on its way. She'd peppered Ian with business questions relentlessly over the last week, and he'd walked her through the processes she'd need to take to get everything started.

Sara had moved her necessities into Declan's vacant rental house on her first night as a free woman. It had been hard for Ian to leave her, but knowing the threat to her life was gone and that Declan was close-by helped ease his apprehensions.

Sara and Addie had become fast friends. Addie had experienced situations similar to those that Sara's mission intended to help. Ian was glad Addie was strong enough to share the toughest parts of her past so that others could find the help they needed.

When their friends began talking amongst each other again, Ian pulled Sara to him and whispered, "You're so beautiful. I can't wait to be your husband."

They'd been praying together regularly for their relationship, but Sara didn't know he'd spent extra time thanking God for this second chance.

Sara nuzzled her face against his chest and said, "What if this is all a dream? It feels too good to be true."

Ian smiled and hugged her tighter. "What if this is just the beginning?"

Epilogue

Addie

Addie clipped the tennis bracelet Declan had given her for their first wedding anniversary on her wrist. The small diamonds wove around her skin in a pattern of triangles that caught the light just right.

A squeal of happiness rang from the living room, and Addie went to see about the fun. The sound of her heels clicking was muffled by the carpet until she stepped to the hardwood of the living room.

"What's going on here?" she asked, eager to know what was causing her daughter to make such a joyful noise.

Suzie sat on the floor, while Declan crept two fingers across the rug toward her. Suzie's shoulders moved up toward her ears as she anticipated the coming tickle hand, and she squealed in delight before her dad even touched her.

Addie clipped an earring in her ear and bent to kiss Suzie on the top of her head. "I love you, my little sunshine." Addie wrapped both hands around her daughter and squeezed before turning to Declan. "You need anything before I go?"

"Just a kiss. You look beautiful," Declan said.

Addie leaned in and planted a sweet kiss on her husband's lips. He smelled like the breakfast he'd cooked earlier—pancakes and bacon.

Declan smiled and rubbed the back of his neck. "We'll be there closer to noon. I'll let her wind down in a minute, and we'll take a nap before we head on over to the church."

Addie smiled and turned to the door. "Have a good time."

"We will. I love you."

"I love you too," Addie said as she closed the door behind her.

Addie started the car with a smile still splitting her face. Suzie was a year old, and Declan had settled into the role of dad easier than Addie could've imagined. He could calm Suzie's cries just by holding her. No words were needed between those two. They had a bond that spoke louder than words.

Declan's own father hadn't been a model for the role, but Declan knew what not to do, and he showed Addie and Suzie how much he loved them every day.

Addie often wished her parents and Declan's mom could be here to see their granddaughter. Suzie was growing so fast. Thankfully, Addie and Declan had a herd of friends who loved their daughter as if she were family.

Pulling out of the driveway, Addie knew her family was taken care of. Now, it was time to help her friend on her wedding day.

Dakota

Lindsey reached both hands behind her back and fumbled for the zipper on her dress.

"Let me." Dakota raced to her and secured the zipper in seconds.

Lindsey stretched her back and turned to him. Her eyes said she was tired, but her smile said she was happy. Dakota knew the pregnancy had been exhausting for her. Emmett was almost two years old, and while he loved working outside with his daddy, he was a mama's boy through and through.

Dakota wrapped Lindsey in his arms, and she melted into him like hot butter. Her growing belly protruded slightly between them. "What can I do to help?"

Lindsey raised her head and widened the smile that masked her pain. "I'd love a cup of coffee, but since I promised myself no caffeine, I'll take a back rub."

Dakota rubbed his hands up and down her back, gently massaging the tense muscles.

Seconds later, Emmett burst into the room. He'd been walking for almost a year, but the eager boy often tripped over his own feet in his haste. He ran to them and wrapped his arms around their legs, joining the family hug.

Lindsey bent down and pulled Emmett into her arms. He wrapped his arms around his mother's neck and squeezed.

Dakota knew Lindsey's back was aching, but she never missed an opportunity to spend the most quality time with their family. He'd known years ago—back in high school—that Lindsey would be a great wife and mom. Holding out for her to come home was worth the suffering he'd put himself through to get back to where he needed to be.

Lindsey tossed Emmett onto the bed, and his laughter echoed through the room.

With her hands on her hips, Lindsey said, "Let's get you dressed, mister." She pointed her finger at him for emphasis. "And don't get your nice clothes dirty. You need to look semi-clean for the wedding."

Lindsey turned to Dakota with a look of worry. "The service is short. We can keep him presentable for twenty minutes, right?"

Dakota shook his head. "It'll be okay. I'll keep an eye on him."

Lindsey linked her hands behind his neck and rested her forehead against his. "I love you. You know that?"

Dakota sighed. "You tell me every day. Do you know that I love you?"

"Of course, I do."

Emmett began jumping on the bed, and Dakota inhaled a deep breath before lifting his head. "I've got him."

Wrapping Emmett in his arms, Dakota hugged his son and said a prayer of thanks to God for giving him a lifetime of happiness.

Jake

Jake sat on the bed and tugged his sock on just as Natalie stomped into the doorway of the bedroom. She was wearing her pajamas, and her hair was unwashed. Jake stood when he saw her chin quiver. She'd been fielding a wide range of emotions with the pregnancy, and he knew sometimes she needed him more than others.

"Whatever it is, it's okay," Jake assured her.

Natalie threw her hands in the air. "We have to leave in forty minutes, and I haven't even started getting ready. I don't know what to wear, and I still need to finish arranging the baby's closet." She let her hands fall dramatically to her sides.

Jake was beside her in seconds. Wrapping his arms around her, he swayed gently from side to side. "It's okay. I promise. I don't care if we're late. Everything is fine."

Natalie's shoulders shook with her sobs, and Jake rubbed his hand over her hair. He wasn't sure what it was like to be pregnant, but he'd seen enough of his friends go through it to know it wasn't a walk in the park. If emotional support was the best he could provide, he'd be sure to give it all he had.

He whispered, "Leave the closet for now, and we'll do it together when we get home this afternoon. You can sit in the rocking chair and point and tell me what to do."

Natalie laughed through the last of her tears and pulled back to look at him. "Okay. That sounds good."

"As for what to wear," Jake continued. "Can I pick out your dress? There's this one I'd really like to see you in today."

Natalie rolled her eyes and wiped her cheeks. "Is it the navy one?"

"Have I told you enough how much I like that one?"

She laughed and pushed his chest playfully. "Only when you ask every Sunday morning if I'll be wearing it to church."

"I'm glad I've made myself clear."

Natalie turned toward the bathroom, but Jake grabbed her hand.

"Wait."

She turned, and he pulled her in close before brushing his lips against hers. He ran his fingers through her hair as she deepened the kiss.

Suddenly, she was pulling away, and Jake reached to tug her back to him.

"Stop it!" She giggled and swatted his hand away. "I really have to get ready."

Jake released her, and she practically skipped for the bathroom. Life with Natalie would never be boring.

. . .

Tori

Tori stuffed more shirts into the washing machine. How much dirty laundry could five people produce? A lot. Too much, if you asked her.

She yelled toward the laundry room door, "Trey, don't forget to feed Sassy!" The border collie had been Trey's birthday present last year and feeding her was his responsibility. Unfortunately, he needed reminding of the chore more often than not.

"I'm on it!" Trey yelled back from the living room.

Meg barreled into the laundry room just as Tori finished loading the washer.

"Hey, can I go on to the church? Addie is going early, and I want to help too." Meg looked older than her sixteen years, wearing a blush-colored dress with cap sleeves and a billowing skirt.

"Wait just a minute, and I'll ride with you," Tori said. "I just need to call Brandon and get my shoes on."

"I'll meet you in the car," Meg said as her heels clicked down the hallway.

Tori grabbed her phone from the kitchen island and dialed Brandon's number.

"Hey, Tor."

It was nice to hear Brandon sounding happy. There had been a time after his mother died when they'd fought tooth and nail to pull him from the darkness.

"Hey, just reminding you that the service starts at noon."

"I know," Brandon said. "Danielle reminded me. We'll be on our way soon."

Danielle, Brandon's fiancée, was one of Tori's favorite people. That woman kept Brandon on the right path better than anyone, and Tori was happy that Brandon had found someone who would fight for him even when things were tough. Danielle had been a gift from God, sent to pull Brandon from the wreckage his mother left.

"Good. We'll see you there," Tori said as she ended the call with a smile.

She'd dressed, fixed her hair, and applied her makeup earlier. The only thing left was shoes. Bounding up the stairs, she practically jogged toward the closet. Meg was waiting on her.

She stepped into the walk-in closet and found Marcus buckling his belt. He wore navy slacks and a crisp white shirt. His suit jacket hung on a hanger beside him.

Tori was used to seeing Marcus in overalls and covered in dirt, and she always appreciated how well he cleaned up on Sundays, but this was a new level of sophistication she'd rarely seen on her husband.

"Hello, Mr. Hottie." Tori reached for him and pulled the collar of his shirt. He'd even remembered to put the collar stays in.

"Mrs. Hottie," he greeted her as he wrapped his arm around her waist, pulling her close.

"I have to go. Meg is waiting on me, and the boys are riding with you." Tori sealed her lips on his. She let the kiss linger as his hand on her waist gripped tighter.

Tori pulled away and squeaked, "Bye. Love you."

Marcus grinned and picked up his jacket. "Love you too, Angel."

Brian

Brian was adjusting his tie as Emma stepped into the room and twirled in her pink dress. Tulle filled the air around her as her skirt lifted. "Daddy, look at my pretty dress."

"It's gorgeous." He squatted next to her and whispered, "Not as pretty as the girl wearing it."

Emma swished the material of her dress. "You know what I feel like?"

"Chicken tonight?" Brian asked, rhyming playfully the way he knew Emma liked.

His daughter giggled. "No, silly. I feel like a real princess."

Leah stepped into the room wearing a silver dress that hung over the slight swell of her stomach and to the floor. The top was covered in sequins, while the bottom was shining satin.

Brian was often dumbstruck by his wife's beauty, but she'd knocked his socks off today.

Leah adjusted Michael on her hip as she smiled at Emma. "You look so cute, baby. Your shoes are over there by the bed." Leah pointed across the room, and Emma padded over to get them.

Brian stood and opened his arms to take Michael from Leah. "You're beautiful," he assured his wife, but the words didn't feel strong enough to express how pretty she was today or any day.

Leah huffed and passed Michael into Brian's arms. "Emma might feel like a princess, but I'm channeling a buffalo over here." She was only beginning to show, but carrying a baby was no joke.

Brian secured Michael to the side and closed the distance to Leah. He grinned and whispered, "I love you more than all the buffalo."

Leah laughed and swatted his shoulder, but Brian didn't hesitate. He kissed her with all the love and passion he felt for her, blocking out any thoughts of buffalo or other four-legged creatures.

When he pulled away, Leah was smiling with her eyes closed.

"I'll shut up now," she whispered.

Emma returned wearing her sleek white shoes. "All ready!"

Brian asked, "Emma, if you're a princess, what does that make Mommy?"

"A queen," Emma said with awe.

Leah grinned and rolled her eyes. "Well, what does that make you?" she asked Brian.

Brian winked at Leah before turning to his son resting on his hip. "It makes me blessed."

Sissy

Lydia raised her arms, and Sissy slipped the dress over her daughter's head. "There. All done," Sissy said.

Lydia had insisted on shoes first, so the only thing left was to secure her hair with a bow.

Tyler wrestled with Jace where the baby lay on the bed. Tyler growled through gritted teeth, "Hold still. You're like a worm."

"You know that's a bad idea," Sissy whispered sweetly into Tyler's ear as she hugged his back.

"What? Getting frustrated? I'm aware of that."

Sissy laughed. "No. Overalls. It's hard to change a diaper in those things. You have to take *everything* off."

Tyler looked down at Jace. He had one leg in the overalls, and Tyler seemed to be deciding if he was committed or if it was easier to abandon the task.

"Here." Sissy reached for Jace's leg. "Let me."

Tyler stepped back and lifted his hands in surrender. "You're the boss." He swept Lydia up into his arms, and she let out a giggle. "You're so pretty."

"Thanks, Dad."

Sissy picked up Jace and turned to grab a different outfit for him from the closet. "You like these pants, cutie?"

Jace just squealed, and she made her way back to the

bed where she slipped the pants on him and kissed his head. "All done for this one too." She lifted him onto her hip and turned to Tyler and Lydia to find them whispering secrets in each other's ears.

Tyler stood from where he'd crouched and took Jace from Sissy.

"You ready?" she asked.

"Is it okay if I admit I'd rather be fishing?"

Sissy grinned. "I love your honesty, but unfortunately, it doesn't change anything." She leaned in and planted a kiss on Tyler's cleanshaven cheek. His skin was warm, and she was reluctant to pull away.

Tyler turned his head and sealed his mouth with hers. Jace tugged on Sissy's hair, and Tyler pulled away with a furrowed brow. "Hey, she's mine too, buddy."

"Don't worry, boys. There's enough of me to go around." She loved her family, but sometimes it was hard to keep her love balanced. She spent most of her time with the kids, but Tyler still held so much of her heart. He worked long hours, and they tended to cling to the moments they were able to spend together.

Her husband rested his hand on the back of Sissy's neck and pulled her in close. "Can we ask Barbara to keep the kids tonight?"

Sissy's smile turned mischievous. "It certainly wouldn't hurt to ask."

Lydia tugged on Sissy's hand. "Come on, Mommy. Let's go."

"Okay. I think we're ready." Sissy was certainly ready. Her family was growing today, and it was about time.

Sara

Sara sat in the music room at the church and dabbed her eye with a tissue. Tori would be upset if Sara cried off the makeup she'd so meticulously applied.

She unfolded the note again and skimmed the words. After reading Mr. Garrison's note to Ian half a dozen times, she knew the contents by heart. Still her heart was eager to read them again.

Mr. Garrison and Ian had been close, and the old man had understood Ian's internal struggle better than most. The words were filled with love and a desire to help. Not many people were lucky enough to have someone in their life that cared if they succeeded and found true happiness.

The words rang in her head as she read them on the page.

You don't have to love her again. I know you never stopped. What you have to do is remember someone loves you and open your heart to what God (and I) always planned for you.

It was the only thing Mr. Garrison had ever asked of Ian—that he open his heart to love. It seemed a simple request, but for a wounded heart like Ian's, she knew it wasn't.

Sara lifted her head and folded the paper. She missed Mr. Garrison, and she wished he could be here today to see her and Ian finally seal their vows.

She closed her eyes and breathed deep. "Lord, thank you for bringing me home. Thank you for sending me a wonderful man to love me for the rest of my life. Thank you for sending me more than one guardian when I needed help. I pray that You'll bless my marriage and intertwine Yourself in our relationships so tightly that we couldn't possibly waver from You."

A knock sounded at the door, and Addie stuck her head through the doorway. "It's time."

Sara whispered, "Amen" as she stood and met her friend. Clasping Addie's hand, Sara said, "I'm ready."

Within minutes, she was waiting just outside the double-door entrance with Lindsey's mother who had been helping with the wedding arrangements. "Are you ready?" Kathy asked.

Ian had told her weeks ago that Brian had offered to walk with her down the aisle, but she'd politely declined his offer. She could walk to Ian on her own, just as she had when they were young.

"I'm ready."

Kathy opened the door, and Sara stepped into the aisle. Ian stood waiting for her at the altar, and she sucked in a breath at the sight of him. He was incredibly handsome, and her heart bloomed as she remembered that her husband-to-be was also her best friend. His devotion to her was unfailing, and his faith in God and the wonders He was capable of was growing daily.

Sara's smile spread wide as she took a moment to scan the church. There were dozens of people in the pews, and they were all here to celebrate her union with Ian.

She'd been waiting her whole life for this—a husband who loved her, friends who supported her, and a home that would always be her haven.

The service was beautiful, and there wasn't a dry eye in the sanctuary by the time Brother Jim announced their completed vows. She practically bounced down the aisle next to Ian. This was the first step toward the rest of their lives together.

Ian tugged her into the preacher's office and closed the door. "How does it feel to be Mrs. Hart?"

Sara bounced on her toes toward him, still feeling the elation of the service. "It feels amazing."

Ian wrapped her in his arms and whispered softly in her ear, "Where do you want to go?"

They hadn't planned a honeymoon, but they'd agreed to take a vacation at the end of the summer.

"Home. Take me home."

Other Books By Mandi Blake

Blackwater Ranch Series

Complete Contemporary Western Romance Series

Remembering the Cowboy

Charmed by the Cowboy

Mistaking the Cowboy

Protected by the Cowboy

Keeping the Cowboy

Redeeming the Cowboy

Blackwater Ranch Series Box Set 1-3

Blackwater Ranch Series Box Set 4-6

Blackwater Ranch Complete Series Box Set

Wolf Creek Ranch Series

Complete Contemporary Western Romance Series

Truth is a Whisper

Almost Everything

The Only Exception

Better Together

The Other Side

Forever After All

Love in Blackwater Series

Small Town Series

Love in the Storm

Love for a Lifetime

Unfailing Love Series

Complete Small-Town Christian Romance Series

A Thousand Words

Just as I Am

Never Say Goodbye

Living Hope

Beautiful Storm

All the Stars

What if I Loved You

Unfailing Love Series Box Set 1-3

Unfailing Love Series Box Set 4-6

Unfailing Love Complete Series Box Set

Heroes of Freedom Ridge Series

Multi-Author Christmas Series

Rescued by the Hero

Guarded by the Hero

Hope for the Hero

Christmas in Redemption Ridge Series

Multi-Author Christmas Series

Dreaming About Forever

Blushing Brides Series

Multi-Author Series

The Billionaire's Destined Bride

About the Author

Mandi Blake was born and raised in Alabama where she lives with her husband and daughter, but her southern heart loves to travel. Reading has been her favorite hobby for as long as she can remember, but writing is her passion. She loves a good happily ever after in her sweet Christian romance books and loves to see her characters' relationships grow closer to God and each other.

Acknowledgments

I've been blessed with a wonderful group of cheerleaders who stand beside me and urge me to keep writing. I can't say enough thanks to the people who help spread the word about my books. My sister, Kenda Goforth, has been my best saleswoman since day one. Kristen Behrens of Books.Faith.Love book blog and Kirby of Preppy Book Princess blog have been a blessing as they shout about my books, but I'm also glad we've become friends.

Tanya Smith and Pam Humphrey not only read my super rough drafts, but they give me honest feedback to make each story better. Jenna Eleam is the best at finding the tiny details that I mess up, and my regular newsletters would be riddled with typos without her.

I shouldn't be surprised that each book in this series looks amazing because Amanda Walker always designs a beautiful cover, and Brandi Aquino always formats a lovely book (especially that paperback).

I've made some wonderful author friends in my first year of publishing. Jeanine Hawkins took me under her wing and made me step out of my comfort zone. K. Leah has been a constant friend and an ear to listen. Stephanie Martin and Hannah Jo Abbott have lifted me up off the floor more than once and encouraged me to keep writing when I felt like quitting. I love our writing circle.

It means so much to me that you took a chance on a rookie author and read my book. I love writing, but I love reading and talking about books too. I get so happy every time a reader reaches out to me to talk about the books, so don't be a stranger! I love you all!

Remembering the Cowboy

BLACKWATER RANCH BOOK ONE

They have unfinished business. She just can't remember what it is.

Camille Vanderbilt is headed back home to Wyoming with one goal: find her old best friend and give him a piece of her mind for ghosting her six years ago. She won't let anyone stand in her way... until a car crash causes her to forget almost everything.

Noah Harding let the love of his life slip away, but what choice did he have when her father threatened to destroy his family ranch? When Camille crashes back into town, he'd better brace his heart for impact.

With her memories gone, Camille struggles to figure out who she can trust. Noah's chances of rekindling his lost love are slipping, and the danger to his family still stands.

When the threats are carried out, who will be left standing at Blackwater Ranch?

Welcome to Blackwater Ranch where the Harding brothers fall hard for the strong women who wrangle their hearts.

Remembering the Cowboy is the first book in the Christian Blackwater Ranch series.

Printed in Great Britain
by Amazon